The Divine One

By

Danielle R. Mani

INFINITY
PUBLISHING

Copyright © 2014 by Danielle R. Mani

ISBN 978-1-4958-0059-7 Paperback
ISBN 978-1-4958-0215-7 Hardcover
ISBN 978-1-4958-0060-3 eBook

Printed in the United States of America

Published June 2014

INFINITY PUBLISHING
1094 New DeHaven Street, Suite 100
West Conshohocken, PA 19428-2713
Toll-free (877) BUY BOOK
Local Phone (610) 941-9999
Fax (610) 941-9959
Info@buybooksontheweb.com
www.buybooksontheweb.com

To my husband,
thank you for all your love and support.
And to my four angels, always remember to be kind
and never too busy to smell the roses or give
someone the time of day — for you never
know who might be asking.
With all my love…

Chapter 1

"Old MacDonald had a farm, E-I-E-I-O. And on that farm he had a pig, E-I-E-I-O. With an oink oink here ..." She tried so hard to ignore the squealing pig noises being shouted in her direction, but the acoustics in the gymnasium only amplified the sound. Delilah Simms looked over at her two gym teachers standing in the corner, hoping that they would intervene. Mr. Mayfield and Ms. O'Brien had divided the gym class into four groups to work different parts of the body. Delilah's group was assigned to work their arms; instead, the girls in her group were mocking her with a juvenile song, and no one was doing anything about it. No one. Mr. Mayfield was standing on the sidelines, and every ten minutes or so he looked up and shouted, "Two more minutes, then move to the next group."

With his salt-and-pepper hair and furrowed skin, Mr. Mayfield looked to be in his mid-fifties. You could tell just by looking at him that he enjoyed spending time outdoors and had never invested a cent in sunscreen. Everyone knew that he was counting the seconds until his retirement from James Madison High in June. Every now and then he looked up and shook his head, but he still never said a word about the taunting. Not a word. Delilah bit her bottom lip nearly hard enough to break the skin. Focusing on physical pain helped distract her from the vexatious situation. Extending her arms like an eagle about to take flight and rotating them in slow circles, she gazed dully at Mr. Mayfield as he serenely paced the gym floor. Instead of scolding the girls for their actions, he simply ignored their singing and squeals prompting Delilah to wonder if he even had a conscience. She dropped her arms to her sides and shook them out.

Ms. O'Brien started teaching two years ago. Delilah had the impression that the teacher was also bullied in high school, which wasn't a stretch considering she still received her fair share of abuse from students. With her naturally pinkish complexion and her round face and body, it was easy to see that she was no stranger to derogatory pig comments. Delilah was sure that the oinking would get to Ms. O'Brien, and that she would say something in her defense. But when she looked, all she saw was a smile plastered to Ms. O'Brien's face. Her teacher looked as if she was getting off on the fact that someone else was being compared to a pig and, like Mr. Mayfield, she wouldn't do a thing to stop it. Not a thing.

Gym was the last class of the day. After the bell rang and Ms. O'Brien dismissed the students, Delilah pensively made her way down the hall toward homeroom. As she walked, she could hear them shouting down the corridor.

"Hey, little piggy. Where are you running off to?"

Delilah recognized Rachael's voice right away. There were five girls in the clique that she referred to as the "Imitators." Rachael Nappi was their leader, the one the others emulated. She controlled and manipulated the other girls like a puppeteer. They were afraid of what they would become without her. Rachael was an imitator in her own right, too—she was notorious for taking other people's ideas and pretending that they were her own.

Rachael's voice was irritating, high-pitched, and squeaky. It was almost comical to hear a voice like that spew such venom. Her voice suited her appearance. She had small, mousy features and short dark hair—not quite a pixie cut, but long enough to push back behind her ears. She probably thought that cutting her hair would accentuate her features in a positive way, but in reality it made her look like a pea-head.

"What's the matter? I know you hear me!" Rachael's voice echoed down the hall.

Delilah tried to get lost in a crowd of freshmen to avoid her. Even though she was a senior, she could easily pass for a younger student. She was on the petite side, but curvy where it mattered. She had hazel eyes and long dark hair that she used to enjoy wearing down. Lately, however, she'd been tying it back into a messy bun.

When she got back to homeroom, she quickly packed up her things. The only Imitator she shared homeroom with was Charlotte, and Charlotte didn't usually say a word to Delilah–unless the other Imitators were there.

Charlotte Moy had an angelic face, complete with soft blue eyes and powder-white skin. Her fair complexion never failed to manifest her emotions, a trait that had tormented her since she was a kid. She was always afraid she would blush at an inopportune moment, allowing anyone to read her like an open book. At this moment, Delilah could tell Charlotte was feeling guilty. In fact, Delilah could probably read Charlotte better than anyone else. This was because they used to be best friends.

Delilah Simms's harassment at school started with just the five Imitators, but that number quickly grew as her unpopularity spread like a cancer. Taking the bus home had become a very traumatizing experience. She used to wait at the bus stop feeling like a gazelle on a wide-open plain, surrounded by ravenous lions. One day, after almost getting into a physical confrontation, she decided to switch her bus route. It didn't matter that the new route was much farther from where she lived, she had to cut through a large park, cross a busy highway on an overpass, and walk five more blocks to get home. Although her new route was a pain to travel, Delilah knew it was better than the alternative. Soon the balmy October weather would turn, and she dreaded the cold winter months ahead.

Today there was a chill in the air. As she walked, Delilah crossed her arms over her chest, shielding her body against the cool air. She could hear children playing in the distance. There was a small part of her that envied them. They sounded so happy, carefree, optimistic — Delilah was devoid of these emotions.

Delilah lived in Queens, New York, on a moderately quiet street. At night when it was peaceful, she could hear the distant sound of the train. Since it was only a twenty-five-minute train ride into Manhattan, she would sometimes travel there on weekends, content just to walk around Times Square or window-shop on Fifth Avenue.

Her house was light blue with black shutters. Her parents bought it when she was just six months old. Sometimes she imagined what her parents were like when they first bought the house — a young couple optimistic about their future, anxious to spend their lives together creating happy memories. Unfortunately, she knew life didn't always turn out as planned.

As she turned the key to her front door, she could hear her mother calling from the kitchen, "D, is that you?" Her mother had called her "D" for as long as she could remember.

"Yes, Mom, it's me." The house was small, and Delilah remembered what her mother once told her about when she and Delilah's father, Joe, first saw the real estate agent's ad for the house. The ad described the house as being "cozy," which her mother said was code for tiny. A long entry hall extended from the front door. To the right was the kitchen, and in the kitchen there was a small door that led to the basement. The basement was supposed to be Joe's man cave, but little by little her mother, Susan, took it over. In retrospect, Delilah wished she hadn't done that; maybe things would have turned out differently. Next to the kitchen was the all-purpose living-office-dining room. In the center of the room there was a large round walnut dining table that used to belong to Delilah's grandmother. Susan took the table after her mother died, saying that she had too many fond memories eating her mother's cooking on that table to ever part with it.

Past the living room, there were three bedrooms. The smallest bedroom used to belong to Delilah's little sister, Darcy. After the accident, Susan put a lock on the door and expected everyone to pretend as though it was no longer there. Delilah and Joe tried to convince Susan to move, but she always had the same excuse. Six months ago Joe got tired of asking her to move and packed his own bags. He now rented a studio apartment about a mile away. Delilah visited him a couple times a week, but she tried not to stay too long because it depressed her. Delilah didn't think her mother would ever give in and sell the house. She knew Susan was convinced that Darcy's spirit was still there.

"How was school today, D?"

"It was OK," Delilah said, tossing her book bag on the floor and kicking off her shoes. Delilah hadn't told Susan the full extent of the trouble she'd been having at school; Susan wasn't even aware that she was now taking a different bus route home.

It would only make her mother nervous if she knew that Delilah had been walking through the park alone. A few years earlier it was all over the local papers that a young woman had been raped while jogging in that same park.

"What do you think about ordering a pizza for dinner tonight?" Delilah's mother asked, trying to force a smile.

Even though she was not in the mood for pizza, Delilah smiled back and said, "Sounds good." These days she tried not to say anything that might upset her mother, who had seemed even more stressed since Joe left. Delilah could see the toll it was taking on her mother whenever she looked in her eyes. She once heard someone say that the eyes were the windows to a person's soul. Her mother's eyes used to sparkle, but now they looked dull and lifeless.

Susan used to be an attractive woman, always getting compliments on her figure, but lately she had become too thin. Delilah tried encouraging her to eat more—she even tried to take up baking, but almost burned the house down one day while attempting to make brownies.

Delilah looked over at her mother standing at the kitchen counter sorting through the mail. Her thin, bony hands compulsively shuffled through the envelopes.

"Mom, I have to run down to the store for something. I'll be back in a little bit." Delilah caught another glimpse of her mother's gaunt frame as she walked toward the front door. After staring at her mother, Delilah decided to surprise her with something sweet for dessert tonight. *Maybe I'll buy her two éclairs*, she thought to herself.

Noticing her pedicure from a few days earlier, Delilah grabbed a pair of flip-flops from the hall closet, thinking her feet looked respectable. She chose candy apple red for her toenails because she thought it made her feet look sexy—if it was possible for feet to look sexy. She took the rubber band out of her hair and gave her head a quick shake. She had almost forgotten how much she liked wearing her hair down. She grabbed her blue windbreaker and keys before running out the door.

Everything in the coffee shop looked so delish. Delilah quickly tried to decide what she should get for herself before the man in front of her finished paying.

"What can I get you?" A woman who looked as if she hated the world greeted Delilah.

"I'm still making up my mind. Everything looks really good," Delilah said, hoping the compliment would soften her up a bit.

"If you don't know what you want, move to the side and let the other customers order," the woman said impatiently.

"I think you should go with the jelly." Delilah heard a man's voice whisper close to her ear. A strange feeling came over her, and she could feel the small hairs on the back of her neck stand up. She didn't bother turning around.

"I'll just have one éclair and one jelly," she said.

"That'll be $2.50," the woman behind the counter said. Delilah reached into her windbreaker and pulled out an empty pocket. She immediately started to sweat realizing that she used the vending machine at school today to buy a bottle of water and a snack. Since she stopped eating in the cafeteria to avoid even more drama, the school vending machine had become her lifeline.

"Um, you know what? I just realized that I forgot my wallet. I'll come back in a few minutes," she said in a whisper, hoping the guy behind her wouldn't hear and the lady behind the counter wouldn't rip her head off. She quickly turned around expressionless, and headed for the door. She didn't look back to see who it was that was standing behind her in line.

Just as she was about to cross the street, her heart nearly stopped as she heard a voice call out, "Excuse me!"

She knew right away that it was the voice from behind her in the coffee shop. She turned around slowly, doing her best to look nonchalant. "Are you talking to me?" she asked, trying to sound aloof.

"Yes, hi! I was just standing behind you in line a couple of seconds ago and I think you forgot this," he said, holding up a small, greasy brown paper bag.

"I didn't buy anything," she answered, trying to avoid eye contact.

"Please just take the bag," he said kindly.

Still looking down, she reached out and took the bag. Peeking inside, she saw one jelly doughnut and one éclair.

"I hate when that happens to me. You know, when you get to the register and you're short on cash." His voice sounded so sincere.

Apparently her attempt to be discreet at the register was futile. Just as she was about to tell him thanks, but no thanks, he looked up and they made eye contact for the first time. He stood at about six feet tall with light brown hair and the bluest eyes she'd ever seen. Oddly, instead of his good looks increasing her discomfort, Delilah felt immediately at ease and simply said, "Thank you."

As the words were coming out of her mouth she couldn't believe that she was saying them. Normally, she would be so embarrassed that she would say something sarcastic and walk away.

"Don't worry about it. You can get me next time," he said.

"Sure," she agreed, standing there staring at him. His snug-fitting, powder-blue T-shirt made the blue in his eyes really pop. He had on dark blue jeans and a pair of really white sneakers that looked as though they had never been worn. "I don't know what I was thinking," Delilah continued with a smile. "I should have checked my pockets before leaving my house."

"No big deal. It happens from time to time."

"Well, I really do appreciate it," she said flirtatiously.

"Okay, well, maybe I'll see you around."

"Yes," she said, flipping her hair with her hand and smiling. He looked at her with an ambiguous grin before he turned and walked away.

As Delilah put the key in her front door, she had a really weird feeling. In fact, she had no idea how she made it home. The entire walk was a complete blur. She remembered her father describing something like this happening once while he was driving home from work. He thought he was having a stroke. She tried to put his mind at ease, explaining to him that it sounded like his subconscious mind was driving the car while his conscious mind was probably thinking about something else. She had heard something similar once while watching the *Dr. Phil Show*. She guessed her explanation made sense to him, because he seemed to calm down after hearing it.

"Hey, you're back already?" Delilah heard Susan's voice coming from the kitchen.

"I went to the coffee shop to get you one of those éclairs that you like so much," Delilah exclaimed, expecting her mother to be delighted by what a thoughtful daughter she had.

"D, it's bad enough that I'm having pizza tonight. There's no way that I'm having an éclair, too." *Really?* Delilah thought to herself.

"Do you know how much sugar is in an éclair?" her mother snapped.

"Well, I didn't think they were a health food," Delilah said sarcastically.

"I'm sorry, D. I really appreciate the gesture. It's just that you know how I like to watch what I eat. At my age you can innocently eat one slice of cheese pizza and one doughnut, and you're off to the cardiologist having one of those angioplasty things."

Susan had a convenient way of pretending to be older than she was just to prove a point. She would pick up Delilah's dirty clothes from the bedroom floor and complain, "My back isn't what it used to be—I can't be picking up your dirty laundry forever," even though Delilah was capable of doing her own laundry and never asked for her mother's help. Susan voluntarily did a lot for everyone and then complained about it. She was something of a martyr.

At first, Delilah planned on telling her about the guy from the coffee shop. She wouldn't normally talk to Susan about stuff like that, but lately she had no friends to confide in. After her mother's unappreciative response to her thoughtful gesture with the éclair, she didn't feel like telling her anything. Delilah thought it was probably for the best, though, because Susan had an annoying habit of picking the most trivial detail from a story and harping on it. If Delilah did tell her about what happened, it wouldn't matter to her mother that Delilah might have just met the man of her dreams; instead, Susan would nag her about the importance of carrying enough money.

She could just hear her: "D, you should always carry at least twenty dollars on you at all times in case of an emergency." Even if her mother made a good point, her points always derailed Delilah from what she was trying to say in the first place, and she would walk away from their conversations feeling completely frustrated.

Delilah decided not to ruin their dinner together. She helped her mother finish setting the table and didn't say anything about what happened at the coffee shop. She had set the table countless times since her father moved out, but she still couldn't get used to laying only two places. She opted to use paper plates and plastic cups for easy cleanup, as she wasn't a big fan of washing dishes.

When the pizza finally arrived, Delilah and her mother sat down to eat.

"So, how's school going? You don't talk much about it these days." Susan said, wiping some pizza grease from her chin.

"Because I would rather not talk about it," Delilah said indifferently.

"Any new boy prospects?" her mother asked.

"Mom, I really don't want to have anything to do with anyone at my school ever again. I'm counting the days to graduation, and then I'm moving away to college." At the mention of moving away, she could see her mother's face tense up. *Maybe I shouldn't have said that.* Delilah really hated the idea of leaving her mother alone. Most of the time she couldn't even think about college; it was hard enough for her to imagine getting through high school.

Although Delilah hated the way she was feeling, she knew that she wasn't alone. She had read countless magazine articles about students who tried to take their own lives—and about some who succeeded—just because they couldn't deal with the torment of high school any longer.

For a moment her mind shifted to her friend, Damon. Damon and Delilah met in Spanish class when they were freshmen. They spent an entire semester passing notes to each other, which was probably why she only knew about three Spanish words. Damon was openly gay, and no one at school seemed to have a problem with it. That's why everyone was so shocked when they heard that Damon hanged himself with a belt in his bedroom closet. Unfortunately, Damon's parents did have a problem with him being gay, but no one knew about it until it was too late.

Delilah had also gone down a bad path a few months ago. She was ashamed to think of it now. Not only was she dealing with problems at school, but she was also having her share of problems at home. She experienced a really weak moment shortly after her father moved out. Susan was going off on one of her rants about communicating with Darcy in the afterlife, and Joe just couldn't take it anymore. Every time Delilah heard them fighting, she blamed herself. She was aware that her parents knew she was the one responsible for Darcy's death.

"D, are you all right? You look like you're a million miles away." Without waiting for a response, Susan continued. "Anyway, I think it's very commendable that you want to focus on college, but please don't let anyone take away your special high school moments. You should be thinking about fun things like your senior prom."

I can't believe she even said the P word, Delilah thought. She had finally made peace with the idea of not going to her senior prom. *Why did she have to bring that up?* "I've told you a million times that I don't want to go to prom and I don't want to walk at graduation. I just want my diploma mailed to me."

"D, honey, I know how you're feeling betrayed and hurt right now, but please don't let these girls get the better of you. You don't want to look back when you're old like me and have regrets."

"Mom, let's just drop it," Delilah said, taking one last gulp of her iced tea.

"I just worry about you. I want you to be happy."

"Then just leave this alone," Delilah said crushing the plastic cup in her hand and walking toward the garbage can.

"Are you sure that you don't want any more pizza?" Susan said, trying to change the subject.

"No, thank you."

"Then have your doughnut. I can put on some tea and we can talk."

The thought of touching a doughnut made Delilah feel sick. "No thanks, Mom, I just want to finish my homework, take a shower, and get to bed."

"OK, I'll finish cleaning up. I'll wrap the rest of those slices in some foil so your father can—" she stopped herself. "Force of habit," she said, looking up teary-eyed. "I keep thinking that he's going to walk through that door."

"I'm sure he'll come home again soon. He probably just needs some time alone," Delilah said, trying to sound optimistic.

As Delilah walked back to her room, she thought about how her dad better come home soon. The last time she went to visit him she noticed that he was acting strangely. It reminded her of an article she read in *Cosmopolitan* that said when a man was cheating he might start to exhibit certain behaviors. One of the things it mentioned was that he might start worrying about his appearance more. He may buy new clothes, start wearing a new brand of cologne, or restyle his hair, which in her father's case wasn't necessary because he was bald. Another thing she remembered reading was that a man may start to hide things like his cell phone from his wife, in case he receives messages, texts, or misses calls from the other woman. *Note to self: if Dad starts sporting a new wardrobe, wearing different cologne, or hiding his cell phone, he's probably messing around.*

Later that night, after she showered and dried her hair, Delilah thought about the mystery man she met earlier. She wondered what his name was and wished that she had someone to discuss it with. She felt so lonely. Usually Charlotte would be the first person she would call about something like this. Things were never the same between the two of them after they started high school and became friends with the Imitators. Delilah wished they had never met Rachael Nappi. She was a jealous, evil girl who would do almost anything to get her way.

Delilah began to think back to when everything started to go downhill. With a tendency to replay things over and over again in her mind—an unhealthy habit that often brought on panic attacks, she ruminated over the details of her high school drama, and came to the same conclusion that she always did. The only person she had to blame for this whole situation was herself.

Chapter 2

BEEP-BEEP-BEEP. Delilah woke from a sound sleep hearing her alarm go off. She'd been meaning to get a new alarm that could wake her with the soothing sounds of nature instead of jolting her out of bed every morning with her heart in her throat. To make matters worse, she usually hit the snooze button at least five times just to muster enough energy to climb out of bed. It seemed so hard for her to start each new day. *What the hell do I have to look forward to?* Delilah thought to herself as she ripped the covers off her body, threw her legs over the side of the bed, and felt around for her slippers.

"D? D, honey, are you up yet?" Delilah heard her mother calling. Before leaving for work, her mother liked to check that Delilah was out of bed. She worked as a secretary for a malpractice attorney about ten minutes away. Even though working in the city would mean more money, she wanted to stay local so she could be closer to her family. Delilah's mother knocked on her bedroom door.

"Come in," Delilah said groggily.

"What's the matter?" her mom asked, poking her head through the door. "You don't feel like going to school again?"

"No, I don't feel like going to school!" Delilah said in a condescending tone as she walked to her closet and swung open the door. Feeling a swell of tears come over her, she tried to bury her face in a fleece robe that was hanging on a hook in her closet.

"D, are you okay?"

"Yes," she said with a quavering voice. She stuck her head further into the closet and pretended to look for a blouse.

"You're not okay. Could you please look at me?" her mother pleaded.

Delilah wiped her hands over her face and turned toward her mother. Without quite making eye contact, she stared at the floor unable to stop the flow of tears beginning to stream down her face.

"My God. What are they doing to you?" her mother asked, sounding distressed. "I'm going to school to talk to your principal to see what he can do about this. If that doesn't work, I'll go over his head and contact the superintendent. I will do whatever it takes to make this problem go away." Her mother tried to sound reassuring.

Delilah didn't want to burst her bubble, so she refrained from telling her how the superintendent could care less about her problem.

"Please don't say anything about this," Delilah said as she sat on the edge of her bed. Her mother walked over and sat down beside her, closed her eyes, and took a long, deep breath.

"D, the more I think about it, I don't want you going to school today. You can stay home until I can figure out a way to make things better for you, okay? And I don't want you to feel bad about this. It's very common for teenagers to have problems. Do you remember what your grandmother used to call the teen years?"

"Yes, I remember. She called them 'tears,'" Delilah said with a smirk.

"That's right. She used to say in her raspy voice, 'take out the double e, n, and y, and that summarizes what those years are really about.' Your grandmother certainly had some convoluted logic, but there was always a bit of wisdom in everything she said," Susan giggled. "D, you will get through this. Life will go on."

"I'm not so sure. It's just really hard for me right now and I'm sorry if I can't be that optimistic," Delilah cried.

"Well, I've made up my mind. You're not going to school today, and I'm not so sure about tomorrow either. Let me see what I can do. I have to go to work now, but I don't want you worrying about this. Why don't you go for a walk and try to clear your head? It's supposed to be beautiful today — around seventy degrees." She bent down and kissed Delilah's forehead. "I love you, honey, and I'm not going to let anything happen to my child. Not again."

As Susan turned to leave the room, Delilah could tell her mother's mind was someplace else. She knew that she was thinking about Darcy and the morning of the accident. Suddenly Delilah felt a pang of guilt that she quickly tried to replace with relief that she didn't have to go to school.

Delilah took her mom's advice and got out of the house. She decided to go for a jog in the park. Wearing her black tight-fit training capris, a white ribbed tank, and her hair tied back in a low ponytail. It felt good being outside in the fresh air. Delilah couldn't help but wonder what she would be doing if she were in school at that very moment. Delilah thought of her school as a prison, and today she was an inmate out on parole. The air somehow smelled sweeter. She lifted her head up toward the sky and let the sunshine hit her face.

Before she started to run, she stood along the side of the track and stretched her arms and legs. She could hear Mr. Mayfield's voice in her head stressing the importance of stretching the hamstring muscles before running. That was probably the only useful tip he had ever given her.

As Delilah stretched, she noticed a couple of guys staring at her from the bleachers. Immediately, she looked away not wanting to invite any unwanted attention. She started walking slowly around the track and then increased her speed to a brisk walk; halfway around the track, she started to run.

Her thoughts turned to school, the Imitators, her parents, and her sister. Her mind began to race. The faster her mind raced, the faster she ran. Delilah could hear her heart pounding in her ears. It was almost like she was trying to outrun her own thoughts—a battle her mind always won. She slowed down to catch her breath. Stepping off the track onto the grass, she put both hands on her thighs, swinging her head down between her legs. As she tried to catch her breath, she looked up and noticed that the two men on the bleachers were still staring at her. Feeling uncomfortable, Delilah decided to get back on the track with the other runners. She tried to ignore the men, but with her peripheral vision she saw one of them stand up.

God I hope he's not coming down here. Just in case, she sped up her brisk walk to a trot and then to a jog again, hoping this would deter him. No such luck.

"Hey, slow down!"

She heard a man's voice calling and she knew that he was talking to her.

"Do you mind if I join you?" A guy who looked like he was in his late thirties asked as he ran up alongside her.

"That's okay," she said, trying to sound more out of breath than she really was, "I like to run alone."

"My friend and I have been admiring you, and he said he didn't think I had the nerve to come over here and talk to you, so I had to come over and prove him wrong. You know how it is."

"Don't you think you're a little old for games?" Delilah quipped, sounding annoyed.

"No! Why? How old do you think I am?" he asked, sounding insulted.

She decided to be kind, "Twenty-eight?" Although he really looked like he could be pushing forty.

"No, I'm a little bit younger than that," he said with a smirk. *Is this guy for real?* She thought to herself. *I can see the gray hair in his cheesy mustache.*

"Honestly, it doesn't really matter to me how old you are. I just want to continue my run. Have a nice day!" she said, hoping the guy would take the hint and get lost. She ran faster.

"Couldn't you stop running for just a little while? I want to get to know you better," he said, trying to keep pace beside her.

Delilah started to feel uncomfortable. *This is just my luck. The day I decide to cut school I'll end up being attacked by this guy and his weirdo friend. I wonder if the man who raped that woman a few months ago had an accomplice.*

"Hey, slow down," he called out as he continued to follow her.

"I need to get out of here," Delilah said under her breath. She took a quick look around the park, trying to get an idea of who was there. She looked for a police officer just in case these guys tried to pull something. She didn't see any, but she noticed a couple sitting on a blanket having a picnic. *They look normal,* she thought to herself. *Maybe I can pretend that I'm with them. I wonder how they'd react if I just plopped down on their blanket and popped a potato chip in my mouth.* Delilah quickly made the decision to stop running and look the jerk right in the eyes. "Please just leave me alone! I really don't want to have anything to do with you!"

"Come on, just—" He was suddenly interrupted by a voice that she recognized.

"I think she's trying to tell you to get lost, so why don't you just walk away before you cause a scene?"

Delilah instantly realized that it was the same voice she heard in the coffee shop. She turned around slowly and saw her mystery man standing there. She never did get his name, but he looked even better than she remembered.

"It's you!"

Without acknowledging Delilah he continued, his eyes fixed on the stalker. "I've been jogging around this track for a while now, watching what's been going on, and it's obvious, dude, that this girl is just not into you."

"Who the hell do you think you are, talking to me like that? When I want dating advice from you, I'll give you a call."

"Sorry, man, you're not getting my number either. I guess you just struck out twice."

"You know what?" the jerk continued, "I've had enough of this. You want her? She's all yours. I really prefer blondes, anyway."

"Then today must be your lucky day. The park is filled with people walking their golden retrievers. Why don't you run along and see if you can come on to one of them?"

Delilah couldn't help but giggle out loud. *Sense of humor: check!* The stalker mumbled something inaudible under his breath before walking away. Without skipping a beat, Delilah's mystery man turned to her. "So, we meet again!"

"How did you ... I mean ... where did you ...?" She had trouble finding the right words.

"I noticed you earlier on the side of the track, stretching—smart move, by the way. It's really painful to pull a hamstring," he said with a smile. "I was about to jog over to say hi, but then I saw that guy come up to you. I thought maybe you knew him, and I didn't want to interrupt. After a little while, though, I could tell what was going on. That guy was relentless, huh?"

"I know. He really freaked me out. Thank you so much for stepping in."

"No problem. I guess I'm a handy guy to have around," he said confidently.

"That's right. This is the second time you've helped me out," Delilah said in a way that made it sound like she hadn't thought about their first encounter until now. *Little did he know that moment was the highlight of my year thus far*, she thought.

"I didn't catch your name the first time," he said. Delilah stared up at him for a moment, mesmerized by his eyes. "So, what is it?"

"What's what?" Delilah asked as if a hypnotist just snapped his fingers and brought her back to reality.

"Your name?" he asked again coyly.

"My name?"

"Yes, your name."

"I'm sorry. It's Delilah, but some people call me D."

"That's a cute name. It suits you well. So, if you give me your number, I can store it in my cell under Delilah," he said, winking.

"I like how cleverly you worked that in," she said, trying to match his confidence.

"Worked what in?" he asked innocently.

"Getting my phone number. You have to admit that you move fast. I still don't even know your name," she said with a grin.

"What do you mean, 'move fast'? I've been kicking myself for not getting your number when we first met. I have no intention of making the same mistake twice."

Man, he's good. She decided not to make it too easy for him. She imagined a guy like this probably got bored quickly, so she decided to have a little fun. "Hey, just because you helped me out—"

"Twice," he interrupted her with a grin.

"As I was saying, just because you helped me out *twice*, doesn't mean that I am willing to give you my number just yet. I still don't even know your name."

"River."

"What?" she asked, confused.

"My name is River."

"Oh," she said, sounding surprised. "That's different."

"So, are you in college?" he asked.

How do I play this? Delilah thought to herself. She would love to tell him that she was in college; she wished she were. But one lie usually just leads to more lies, so she thought it best to go with the truth. "I'm still a senior in high school. I was a little under the weather this morning, so I decided to take the day off."

"I'm sorry to hear that. I hope you're feeling better now," he said, sounding sincere.

"I'm feeling a lot better, thank you. So what's your story?" she asked, trying to take the focus off of herself.

"What do you mean, 'my story'?"

"Tell me about yourself. Do you go to college?"

"Yes, I go to college in Florida. I'm pre-law."

"Studying to be a lawyer. No wonder you argued so well with that guy."

"Arguing is my biggest motivation for wanting to become a lawyer—I just love it," he said seriously. Delilah looked at him skeptically.

"I'm kidding," he said with a smirk. "But I do believe in arguing when it pertains to seeking justice."

Truth, justice, and the American way. Maybe this guy is Superman.

"So what brings you to New York? Shouldn't you be reading a law book under a palm tree somewhere?" Delilah joked.

"I decided to take a semester off. My uncle's law firm is working on a big case, so he asked that I come up here and help out for a while."

"That's a good idea. I'm sure you'll learn more working with him than you ever would from a book."

"I hope so, but in reality I'll probably just be doing a lot of filing and making copies—that kind of stuff."

"Well, you have to start somewhere," Delilah encouraged. "When do you think you'll be going back to Florida?"

"I'm not sure yet. There are quite a few things I have to do in New York first and, who knows, if I end up liking it here, maybe I'll stay." Delilah couldn't believe how absurdly happy she was to hear that.

"That would be nice. I think you'd really like living in New York," Delilah said casually.

"Well, if you ever decide to give me your number, I could give you a call and maybe take you to the city for dinner sometime?"

This was the first time she'd ever been asked out on a real date. For most of the guys she knew, a date was making out in their parents' basement.

"I'd really like that," she said.

"So would I." River smiled and looked at his phone. "Oh, great," he said sarcastically.

"What's the matter?"

"My phone just died. My charger is in my car."

"Why don't we just do it the old-fashioned way and use paper and a pen?" she asked.

He laughed. "I think we sometimes complicate things with all the technology. I do have a pen in my car. I drove up from Miami. It took more than twenty-four hours, but it's been worth it just to have my own car. I didn't want to rely on borrowing my uncle's. I'm parked in the lot behind the track. Do you want to take a walk with me?"

Delilah hesitated for a moment—without realizing why. "I'll walk over with you." She was curious to see what kind of car he drove, among other things.

They passed plenty of empty spots as they walked toward his car. River must have known what she was thinking because he said, "I always like to park my car away from the other cars. It keeps it from getting dinged."

When they got to his car, she saw that it wasn't really a car at all, but a Jeep. It was even nicer than she imagined. It fit him perfectly—sporty and neat. As he pulled his keys out of his pocket, he dropped them on the floor. He looked up at her and said, "Butterfingers." That's the last thing Delilah remembered before she screamed.

Chapter 3

Everything seemed to happen very fast. Delilah instinctively reached for the brick that he used for the attack. It was covered in blood. She smashed him on the side of the face with it.

"Help! Someone, please help!" Delilah screamed as loud as she could. Looking around, she saw a cop car in the distance. She continued to scream and wave her hands. Suddenly, she heard a siren, which got louder as the police car came closer. Normally the sound of police sirens would make her nervous, but right now it was the best sound in the world. An officer drove up, practically smashing into the Jeep. For a moment, Delilah noted the irony. She and River had just discussed the precautions River takes to keep his Jeep from getting dinged.

"Miss, are you all right?" asked the officer, who looked like he was in his late forties.

"Yes," Delilah said. She realized for the first time that she was crying. "I'm fine. It's my friend that needs help. "River, River, can you hear me? Please answer me."

"What happened to your friend, Miss?" The officer asked, hitting the receiver attached to his lapel. "This is Officer McCarthy at Cross Bay Park. I'm going to need an ambulance and some assistance over here at the back of parking lot B." He looked back at Delilah. "So what happened to your friend?" Delilah paused for a moment, wondering if he'd let her answer this time.

"He ... he was attacked!" she exclaimed, sobbing. "These t ... two guys who were trying to talk to me before, they came out of nowhere and hit him with a brick. I ... I was able to pick up the brick—one of them dropped it—and I hit him in the side of the face with it before he took off. I think I was able to get in a good shot."

"So you know who these guys are?" the officer asked.

"Yes, they tried to hit on me while I was jogging," Delilah said. *Who could forget that cheesy mustache?* She thought.

Delilah knelt down behind River, holding his head in her hands. She kept telling him that he would be okay when, suddenly, she noticed his eyes open.

"River, can you hear me?"

"Yes. What the hell happened?" he asked hazily.

"Remember that guy you spoke to on the track?"

"Yeah."

"He and his friend must have followed us to the parking lot, and they hit you with a brick when your back was turned," Delilah explained, fighting back more tears.

"They sound like real tough guys, hitting a man when his back is turned," the officer said, sounding disgusted.

"Help me up. I have to find them. I just want to get my hands on those sons of bitches." He tried to get to his feet, but stumbled back and almost fell, prompting the officer to catch him.

Delilah bent down to pick up his keys from the ground, and clicked the fob to unlock the Jeep. She and the officer led River to the passenger side and settled him in the seat. "Just sit and try to relax until the ambulance gets here," Delilah tried to calm him.

"What ambulance?" River asked.

"I called an ambulance. You need help. You probably have a concussion," the officer stated.

"I'm fine. I just need a couple of minutes to compose myself."

"I feel awful. This is my fault," Delilah said, with tears streaming down her face.

"Please don't cry, Delilah," River said.

Delilah was comforted by the fact that his memory appeared to be somewhat intact; he hadn't forgotten her name.

"You shouldn't feel bad. That was a brave thing you did, hitting that guy," the officer said with a wink.

"What's this about you hitting that guy?" River asked, looking surprised.

"To be honest, the whole thing felt surreal. I just remember hitting one of them before they both took off running," Delilah explained.

"I suppose that makes you my hero," River said. "They probably weren't expecting you to fight back."

I wish I could fight back like that at school, Delilah thought to herself. She would love to hit Rachael Nappi in the face. Rachael deserved it.

"If you hadn't fought back and yelled for help, those guys might have done a lot worse," the officer said.

"I really didn't think I was capable of something like that."

"I guess you are a lot stronger than you think," River said decisively.

"You should feel proud," the officer added, nodding his head in approval.

"Well, I'm proud of you," River said, taking Delilah's hand.

"Look at you," Delilah interrupted, trying to change the subject. "Your head is still bleeding. Don't you have some tissues or a first-aid kit in this Jeep?"

"You can check my glove compartment. I may have some napkins in there."

"There's nothing in there," Delilah said, bending her head to look inside.

"I may have something in my car," the officer said.

"It's okay. I hear the ambulance now. They'll be able to take care of you," Delilah said unsure whether she was trying to reassure herself or River.

A minute later the officer returned from his car. "Here we go. I was able to find some gauze. Our first-aid kit is almost empty—I couldn't even find a Band-Aid in there. The ambulance will have what you need."

"Wait a minute," River said, taking the gauze from the officer's hand. "I'm not going in any ambulance. I'm fine. I just want to get out of here."

"River, you've just had a really bad blow to the head. You should to go to the hospital just to make sure everything is okay," Delilah protested.

"I agree with your friend here. You really should go to the hospital," the officer said.

"That's really not necessary. I'll just drive back to my uncle's house and lie down for a while."

"River, you're in no condition to drive," Delilah said, sounding a bit like her mother.

"I'm fine," River said as he slid out of the car. He stumbled a bit upon standing and looked like he was going to fall.

"This is ridiculous. If you insist on not going to the hospital, at least let me drive you home. I mean, you can't even stand up on your own. How the hell are you going to drive a car?"

"If you drive me home, who's going to drive your car?" he asked.

Delilah's initial reaction was to tell him that she didn't even have a car, let alone a license. She had taken the road test twice and failed both times. She didn't do well under pressure. This probably wasn't the best time to bring any of that up.

"Sir, the ambulance is here," the officer said as he walked around to the passenger side of the Jeep and tried to open the door.

"I don't need an ambulance," River said abruptly. "Start the car please, I want to get out of here." River sounded anxious.

"Sir, I don't think it's a good idea for you to just leave. You should have that cut looked at."

"That's all right, officer," Delilah interrupted. "I'll make sure that he sees a doctor." The officer gave her a disapproving look, then walked over to the ambulance and stuck his head through the open window. He talked to the paramedic and pointed to them a few times. Delilah didn't know what he was saying, and she didn't wait around to find out. She started the car, put it in reverse, and slammed her foot on the accelerator. If this were her road test, she would have already failed.

Delilah looked at River, who was lying back on the headrest, pressing the gauze tightly to his head. He looked so pathetic and vulnerable.

"Thank you for leaving," he said weakly. "There was no way I was getting in that ambulance."

"So, where does your uncle live?" Delilah asked as she began to drive aimlessly.

"On Park Avenue."

"Park Avenue!" she said, sounding surprised. "What are you doing in Queens?"

"I have a friend who lives near the coffee shop where we met."

"Oh, so that's why you were there," she said, secretly hoping his friend wasn't a girl.

"One day we ran together at Cross Bay Park and I liked it. I'm glad that I decided to come back or else I wouldn't have bumped into you."

"I can't believe you're saying that after what just happened." Delilah said. "So, do you want me to drive you into the city?" she asked apprehensively, knowing that she's not ready to deal with aggressive city taxi drivers.

"Just drive yourself home, and then I'll take the car and drive myself back into the city," he suggested.

"No, I don't want you driving. Not in your condition. Is your uncle home now?"

"My uncle is never home. He's a workaholic."

"How about an aunt or a cousin? You need someone to stay with you. If you do have a concussion, which you probably do, you're not supposed to be left alone."

"I'm fine. Please stop worrying about me. Once I get back to my uncle's, I'll just get a little sleep, and I'm sure I'll feel a lot better in a couple of hours," he said.

"Sleep?" Delilah yelled. "Don't you know that it can be dangerous to fall asleep if you have a concussion? Didn't your mother teach you anything?"

"If you want to know the truth," River said abruptly, "my mother never taught me much of anything. She was a degenerate alcoholic who spent most of her time with her boyfriends."

Delilah was completely taken back by his sudden candor. Maybe he was hit on the head harder than she thought.

"I'm sorry," he apologized realizing he said too much. "I shouldn't have said that. I know you're just trying to help and you don't need to hear about my screwed-up childhood."

"I understand. Why don't you just come to my house? My mom is at work and I can keep an eye on you," she suggested.

"You want to take care of me? That's really sweet."

"Well, it's my fault that you're in this mess, and I'm not going to let you stay by yourself. God forbid something else happens to you. I would never forgive myself."

"I see," he said. "Well I can't have that on my conscience, now can I? I guess I'll just have to cooperate and let you take care of me. I'll try to be a good patient," he said, turning to her and smiling.

Delilah couldn't believe how fast she was falling for him.

Delilah took River's arm and helped him lean on the post outside her front door.

"I'll be okay, really," River said, touching her shoulder as though Delilah were leaning on him instead of the other way around.

"Good afternoon!" an elderly voice yelled out. Delilah turned around to see who it was.

"Good afternoon, Mrs. Johnson," *Just what I need right now, the neighborhood gossip,* Delilah thought to herself. *Don't walk over here. Don't walk over here.*

"Isn't it a beautiful day?" Mrs. Johnson said as she made her way up Delilah's walkway with her dog. "Daisy is so happy to be out walking. It's been so cold that lately I've just been letting her do her business in our backyard. Of course, I'm going to have a bunch of poopy mines in the spring, but with my sciatica being what it is, I just can't walk her all around the neighborhood in the cold weather," she said without taking a breath and without taking her eyes off River.

"I know it has been cold. Well, I guess I'll be seeing you," Delilah said, raising her voice so she could be heard over the barking.

"Daisy? Daisy? What's the matter? Well, that's odd. She never barks like this," Mrs. Johnson said while trying to comfort her dog.

"Maybe she just misses doing her business in your yard," Delilah said, trying to wrap up the conversation. From the corner of her eye Delilah saw River grin. She was glad the dog was barking and acting strangely as it seemed to fluster Mrs. Johnson.

"Well, I better keep on walking because something is bothering my little Daisy-poo."

"Good-bye, Mrs. Johnson, Daisy."

Delilah couldn't believe how Mrs. Johnson treated the eight-pound ball of fur like a child. Delilah liked animals and had always nagged her parents for a pet, but they would never allow it. Her mother used to say that pets don't live long enough, and she wouldn't want to go through the pain of losing one. Delilah thought of the irony in her mother losing Darcy so young. Three years old — the average life span of a hamster.

"Come on, let's get you inside," Delilah said holding the door open for River. "I'll get an ice pack for your head. By the way, I apologize for not introducing you to Mrs. Johnson. It's just that she's sort of the neighborhood busybody, and I didn't want to start explaining ..."

"I understand. Actually, if it's all right with you, I'd like to use your bathroom to wash up."

"Of course, I'll show you where it is."

Delilah walked him down the hall to the bathroom. As soon as he closed the door, she ran into her bedroom and began to clean like she had just polished off a case of Red Bull. She grabbed all the clothes and towels that were piled on top of her dresser and threw them into her closet. She spotted a box of tampons on her desk and immediately tossed it under her bed. As she scanned the rest of her room, she found a bag of pretzels, gum wrappers, a soda can; she never realized what a slob she was. *Note to self: clean room more often.*

She took all the garbage that she compiled and threw it into a shopping bag that was lying on the floor. For the first time in months she pulled the curtains back to let some sunlight in and cracked the window for some fresh air. She wanted her room to feel comfortable and inviting. She wished she had the time to run out and get some fresh flowers, but she settled for spraying a little perfume in the air instead.

Delilah hopped onto her bed and fluffed the pillows. She stayed there for a moment pretending it was the first time she had ever been on her bed. She supposed River would think it was comfortable. As she heard the bathroom door open, she quickly hopped up to check her appearance in the full-length mirror hanging behind her bedroom door. She was pleasantly surprised by how she looked. After all that crying, she thought her eyes would have been puffy. She opened the dresser drawer and quickly rummaged through her assortment of lip gloss. As she stood behind her bedroom door applying it, she could hear what sounded like whispering. She turned her head and held her ear to the door straining to make out what was being said. All she could hear was, "I know. I will." Opening her bedroom door slowly, she saw River standing in the hall.

"Is everything okay?" she asked skeptically.

"Yes, why?"

"I just thought I heard you talking to someone."

"I was. I just called my uncle from my cell. I wanted to let him know what happened."

"What did he say?"

"He just said to take it easy."

"I think that's very good advice," Delilah said taking his hand, leading him toward her bedroom. She was anxious to get him out of the hallway. Her mother had a bunch of pictures hanging on the walls, including photos of her sister, and Delilah just didn't feel like answering any questions about Darcy right now.

"I think you should lie down,"

"Thank you. Your bed is really comfortable," River said, fluffing up the pillow.

"Thanks." Delilah knew he wasn't just being nice. She had to admit that her bed did feel comfortable.

"I'll get you a bottle of water. Would you also like some aspirin?"

"I'll take a couple of Excedrin if you have any. My head is killing me."

"I really think you should see a doctor. It's still early—I can call a doctor right now and make an appointment."

"I'll tell you what," he said, sounding a little less feeble. "If I'm not feeling better by tomorrow morning, I'll go to the doctor then."

I just hope that's not too late! Delilah thought to herself. She immediately felt terrible for thinking so negatively—she was sure River would be fine, but she really liked him, and the more she fell for him, the more she was afraid of losing him.

When she looked in the medicine cabinet, she couldn't find any Excedrin. All she managed to forage were two generic aspirin. She guessed her father bought that bottle. He was always looking to save a buck on the most frivolous things. She thought he could have at least coughed up a few paltry cents for some name-brand aspirin. She hated the idea of handing River these "Pain Away" pills.

When she walked back into her room, she saw River lying on her bed with his eyes closed. "River," she whispered. "River, I have your bottle of water and your aspirin. It's not Excedrin, but I think it should work." She continued talking, but he still didn't answer. "River," she said again a bit louder. *Oh, God, he's not answering me. He probably has a concussion and fell asleep.* She shook his arm.

Looking down at him, all she could think was how hot he looked even when he was sleeping. *What am I thinking? He could be dead!* "River!" she yelled.

He opened one eye. "Got you!" he said with a laugh.

"Do you think that's funny?" she said, annoyed.

"I'm sorry if I scared you," he said as he lifted himself onto his elbow.

"You really freaked me out. I thought you were dead. How do you think that would make me feel? Your blood is on my hands, you know. It's my fault those guys attacked you."

"Stop it. It's not your fault. You can't help it that you were born beautiful. I'm sure men approach you all the time."

He was definitely a smooth talker. She had to give him that.

"Thank you. They don't approach me *all* the time," Delilah said with a smile. She decided to play it cool. Inside, though, she thought how nice it was to hear a compliment. Delilah had almost forgotten that there's a whole wonderful world outside the confines of her high school.

"In all seriousness, how are you feeling?"

"A lot better, thanks to you," he said amorously.

"I'm going to get you an extra pillow so that you can prop your head up a bit more. It might help with your headache."

"I don't need an extra pillow."

"Well, what can I get for you? Do you want me to make you something to eat?"

"Do you know what I think would make me feel better?" he asked gently.

"What's that?" she asked.

"If you come over here and sit next to me. You know I would walk over to you but I'm in so much pain," he teased, pouting his bottom lip.

"I think you're starting to take advantage of my kindness," she said with a smile as she walked over to the bed and sat down beside him. "I'm here now. What do you want?" she said, trying to sound annoyed.

"I just want to tell you something," he whispered.

"Well you're going to have to speak up. I can hardly hear you."

"Come closer," he said.

Delilah couldn't help but smile at him. She leaned her face close to his and whispered back, "What do you have to tell me?" Suddenly she felt his arm reach around her back. He quickly pulled her in close and pressed his lips against hers, kissing her gently. She pulled back from him and smiled.

"River, you should rest," she said standing up, trying to compose herself.

"I'm fine," he insisted.

"You really should see a doctor just to make sure everything is okay."

"I promised you that I would go, and I will."

"I would feel a lot better if I hear a doctor say that you are all right."

"I will go to the doctor tomorrow, but on one condition." He paused for a moment while Delilah waited with baited breath. "You have to come with me." She didn't know why, but she stood there and stared at him.

"Well, what's it going to be?" he asked, teasing.

"Of course I'll go with you. Just let me know what time."

"I was thinking that if I can get an early appointment, and if everything is okay, we could spend the rest of the day together. I really don't think my uncle will mind if I take the whole day off. He and his associates can find someone else to get their coffee."

And I guess the Imitators will have to find someone else to torment tomorrow. As happy as she was to hang out with River tomorrow, she was equally as happy to miss school again.

Chapter 4

The next morning, Delilah was awakened by the sound of Susan's morning routine. She heard the loud squeak of the hot water turning on. Her father was supposed to fix that, but he moved out before he had the chance. Susan always turned on the hot water first, claiming that it took at least ten minutes for it to fully heat up. Delilah had never found this to be true, and she used to argue with her mother about the importance of conserving water. Recently, though, she realized that arguing with Susan about things like that was pointless. After turning the shower on, her mother usually popped a pod into the Keurig and turned on the morning news. Delilah thought her mother's hearing might be deteriorating because of the way she blasted the television in the morning. Placing a pillow over her head, she tried to muffle the sound. She didn't like hearing the news in the morning—most of the time it just depressed her.

River left the house around four thirty yesterday. Delilah asked him to leave before her mother got home from work. She usually got home at five o'clock, but because her schedule fluctuated, she sometimes worked late. Last night she got home after seven. If Delilah had known that she was going to be so late, she would have asked River to stay longer. She couldn't believe how much she enjoyed being with him. The more time she spent with him, the more she liked him. She didn't say anything to Susan last night about River. By the time her mother got home and settled, Delilah could tell that she was really tired and not in the mood to talk about the school situation.

Delilah supposed later tonight she'd tell her mother about River. If she did, she'd conveniently leave out the part about him being at their house. That wouldn't go over well. Her parents would never approve of her being alone in the house with a guy.

Delilah heard the floor creak outside her door; she knew her mother was standing there. She waited for her to knock, but she never did. Delilah was relieved. Having to pretend that she was going to school today would be too much. River was picking her up at nine thirty. He got the earliest appointment they had.

Delilah stayed in bed for about a half hour waiting for her mother to leave. As soon as she heard the front door lock, she got out of bed. For the first time in a while, she was not dreading the day ahead. She was really looking forward to spending the day with River. Before walking over to her closet, she checked the weather forecast on her phone. It was supposed to be in the high sixties with a chance of rain in the afternoon. She decided to wear her favorite pair of jeans. Even though she owned about ten pairs, there was that one pair that just fit her better than all the rest. She only washed them after every other wear for fear they might change shape. Pairing them with a plain white tee seemed like a good plan. For some reason, she always felt most confident in a pair of great-fitting jeans and a tee.

After her shower she pulled her hair into a ponytail so it wouldn't frizz from the humidity, then she applied some makeup. Usually she tried not to wear too much—not that she had anything against wearing makeup, it was just that she thought wearing a lot made her look even younger. It reminded her of a little girl playing dress-up. She dabbed a little concealer under her eyes and over a few imperfections. She followed that with blush and a couple coats of mascara. Finally, she put on her favorite lip gloss. It had such a pretty pink tint, and it tasted like strawberries. She hoped that River wasn't allergic to strawberries. The thought of kissing him again made her stomach flip.

Glancing at the clock, she saw that it was nine thirty on the nose. She was always running late, but not today. She wanted to be waiting outside when he pulled up. She locked her front door, but when she turned around she saw that he was already in the driveway. His window was down and he had a big smile on his face; it must have been contagious, because she could feel herself smiling, too. She walked over to his Jeep and poked her head through the open window.

"You're late," she said.

"It's nine thirty-one," he apologized. "I'll try to do better next time."

"How are you feeling today?" she asked, climbing into his Jeep.

"I feel great, and I think that going to the doctor is a complete waste of time. I'm only going because I promised you yesterday that I would."

"Well, I appreciate that you're keeping your promise to me." *I hope you always keep your promises.* As they stopped at a light, she gently turned his head toward hers and looked at his cut. "You must be a great healer," Delilah said. "I can hardly see the mark."

"I do my best."

Delilah was relieved that they didn't have to wait at the doctor's office too long. In fact, it was a really quick visit. She opted to stay in the waiting room when the nurse called River into the examination room.

"See, I told you that I was fine," River said as they walked back to the car. He walked around to the passenger side and opened the door for her.

"What do you mean? You told me in the elevator that the doctor said you have a slight concussion and that you need to take it easy for a couple of days. He wouldn't say that if he thought that there was nothing to worry about."

"First of all, he said that I should 'try' to take it easy, not that I have to, and I should just try not to concentrate too hard. I'll probably still end up going into my uncle's office to help out, but I'm just assisting—it's not like my tasks require a ton of concentration. The most intellectually stimulating thing I do is make copies."

"I don't think you're giving yourself enough credit. I can already tell that you are bright and motivated, and I'm sure that they'll notice your potential really soon, and—"

River leaned in and kissed her on the lips.

"What was that for?" she said, sounding surprised.

"I didn't mean to interrupt, it was just that you were saying such nice things. Thank you for your confidence," he said while brushing a strand of hair from her eye.

"You're welcome, but I still think that you should take at least one more day off from the office just to make sure you're okay. You can hang out with me," she said with a grin.

"You're probably right," River said with a smirk. "A concussion can be a very serious thing, and my uncle did say that I should take as much time as I need before coming back."

Delilah started to laugh. "I think that's a good idea, but you still have to take it easy. What would you like to do today? It's supposed to rain later, so maybe we can go someplace indoors?"

"Let me think." After a moment he said, "How about the aquarium?"

"I love the aquarium!" Delilah replied excitedly. "That's a nice and relaxing place to visit."

They walked around the aquarium for a while. River seemed really interested in everything they saw, even taking the time to read the little signs hanging beneath the fish tanks.

"Look at this little fish," Delilah said. "He looks like he's smiling at us."

"That's a pinecone fish. It says here that they appear to have a glowing smile, but that's just due to the bioluminescent bacteria inside their mouths," he said, sounding intrigued.

"Maybe you should be majoring in marine biology at college instead of law," she quipped with a smirk.

"I loved biology in high school," he said, scanning some of the other signs. "I was a real nerd. I know it's hard for you to believe," he said flippantly.

"Let me guess, you were a nerd most of your life and you only just started to blossom, so to speak, at around sixteen or seventeen years old? Am I right?"

"I don't know, I guess so. I started to work out more and I suppose I did start dating more. Why, what's your point?"

"Ugly Duckling Syndrome," Delilah sighed.

"What is that?" he asked curiously.

"That's what my friends used to call it when a guy's physical attributes finally catch up to the rest of him. It's a good thing."

"What do you mean?"

"Well, I was wondering how a guy like you can be so—" she hesitated to finish her sentence.

"Go on," he teased.

"Are you really going to make me say it?" she asked.

"Yes, I'm really interested in what you think of me."

"Well, it's just that you seem like a really great guy, and ..."

"Go on," he said while nudging her with his shoulder.

"It's always been my experience that guys who are really sweet and thoughtful are either not that good-looking or gay. The first doesn't apply to you, and you don't seem to be the latter."

"Honestly, I don't think you're that off-base with your ugly duckling theory. I never really dated much in high school. I was genuinely interested in learning; I used to study a lot. It took my mind off other things that I had going on."

Unsure how to respond, Delilah changed the subject. "Are you getting hungry?" she asked.

"I could go for a little something. I'll buy us some lunch and we can sit outside to eat. It hasn't started raining yet. I think I might even have a blanket in the trunk of my Jeep. I can run out to the lot and get it before we get the food."

"That sounds good."

It was such a beautiful day for a picnic. River and Delilah both got grilled chicken salads and fries from the aquarium cafeteria. Delilah felt less guilty about having fries when her main course was only a salad. They picked a great spot on the grass where they could see the penguin exhibit. Delilah wanted to learn more about River's family, but she was unsure how to go about bringing it up. She was waiting for a good time, and sitting in this perfect setting seems just as good a time as any.

"River, can I ask you a question?"

"Yes, and you don't have to be so formal about it—relax." He took her by the arm and pulled her into his chest.

"Well, I was just wondering about your family. You mentioned your mother, but you haven't said anything about your dad."

"That's because I don't see my father anymore. Actually, I haven't seen him in years."

"Why, what happened?"

"He and my mother were never married. They met in a bar where she worked. Apparently they had a one-night stand that resulted in me."

"Well, I'm grateful for that encounter," she said, giving his arm a squeeze.

"Thanks. I'm grateful for it, too. Sometimes I think about how close I came to having never been in this world. It really was a fluke thing. I mean, my parents have absolutely nothing in common. My mother was a complete disaster."

"I'm sure she's not that bad," Delilah said, trying to sound positive. "She must have done something right. Look at how well you turned out."

"Thanks—but don't give her any credit for how I turned out. She didn't raise me."

"Who raised you?" Delilah asked.

"Who raised me?" He repeated her question. "I, uh, have an older half-brother, Josh. I went to live with him when things got really bad."

"What about your dad? What happened to him?"

"My father is a lawyer. The last time I Googled him, he was still working for a law firm in Manhattan."

"Your dad is living here in New York?"

"Yes, he was born and raised in New York. He was in Florida with a friend when he met my mother. I don't know what happened the night he met her, but I'm guessing alcohol played a big role in my conception," River joked.

"You're so bad. You don't know what happened that night."

"I'm just teasing. Although I'm pretty certain that they were both intoxicated. Not to say my father wasn't initially attracted to my mother. I saw pictures of her when she was younger and she was really pretty. She just started to let herself go as the years went on and life got harder. I know that drugs and alcohol played a big role in that."

As River spoke about his mother, Delilah couldn't help but think that the description sounded a bit like her own mother. "Substance abuse can really do a lot to a person's appearance," Delilah said.

"It can do a lot to a person in general," River said. "My mother was always too drunk or too high to show any real emotion. Actually, I take that back. I do remember her always looking really pissed off whenever my father came to Florida to visit. She would stand in the doorway of our dilapidated house, smoking a cigarette, staring at the back of the rental car as my father and I drove away. I would turn around to wave good-bye through the back window, but she never waved back. She always looked so pathetic."

"I'm sure your dad made her feel insecure. Not on purpose, but she probably knew that he could give you a lot of the things that she couldn't."

"I agree, but a good mother would want me to have those things. I always got the impression that she was jealous of his success. I think she was mad that he would buy me things, but never spent a cent on her. I think she was envious of his wife, too. Even though she knew that I had never met her, she would always ask me questions about her, like if my dad talked about her a lot or bought her nice things."

"It sounds pretty sad to me. She probably just wished that she could be with him."

"Then she should have cleaned up her act—not to mention herself and the house—instead of making things harder on everyone."

"I'm sorry River, I didn't mean to—"

"No, I'm sorry," River interrupted. "I'm not mad at you. It's just that every time I speak of my mother, I can't help but feel angry. You know, I used to try and see things from her point of view. I used to actually feel guilty about the gifts that my dad bought me. I would hide them under my bed when I came home so she wouldn't see them and feel bad."

"It's really sweet that you would think about your mother's feelings like that." Delilah reached over and stroked the top of his hand.

"I really wish she would have thought about my feelings sometimes."

"Why? What do you mean?" Delilah asked.

"It's just that sometimes I think that if it wasn't for her, my life—" he paused for a moment. "I just think my life would have turned out different."

"Do you think your life is turning out bad? I mean, if just one thing went differently, you might not be sitting here with me right now." Delilah leaned in and kissed him on the cheek.

"You don't know how lucky I feel to be sitting here with you right now," River said sincerely.

"So what happened with your dad? He sounds like he was a good father. Why did he stop coming around?"

River sat for a minute as if he was reflecting on the question.

"I'm sorry if I'm asking too many questions," Delilah apologized, wondering if she was being too nosy.

"I can remember coming home from school one day," River continued. "I was so excited because my dad was supposed to pick me up and take me to a baseball game. I got ready and sat by the window and waited. I must have sat by that window for hours. Even after the game started, I still waited. It never occurred to me that he wouldn't show. Finally, my mother decided to tell me that she spoke with him earlier in the day and he told her he wasn't coming. He got an earlier flight and he was going back to New York. Then she added, in a very matter-of-fact tone, that he would never come to see me again. She rattled something off about my father's 'real' family finding out about me and that his wife threatened to file for divorce and take him for everything he was worth if he continued to see me."

"River, that's awful. I'm so sorry. Didn't she say anything to try and comfort you?"

"Um, let me think." River took his hand off the blanket, grabbed a clump of grass, and pulled it out of the ground. "Oh yeah, she did say that it was a good thing I didn't go to the game, because my team lost."

"That was it? That's all she said?"

"Yup, she was a real piece of work, my mother."

"So you never saw your father again after that night?"

"That's right."

"Well, if you know your Dad is so close to where you are now why…?"

"Delilah, please just leave this alone. I know that you're just trying to help, but I really have no interest in seeing him. I moved in with Josh shortly after the incident with my dad. You would like my brother and his wife, Marie. They have two little boys: Jack, who's four, and Robert—we call him 'Robbie' — who's two."

"How cute. I would love to meet all of them someday," she said enthusiastically.

"Maybe you will," he said, looking doleful. "Listen, would you mind excusing me for a minute?

I promised my uncle that I would call just to check in and let him know how I'm doing."

"Sure, take your time. I'll just hang out here and relax a bit more."

"If you get bored, have a look at the penguins. I'm sure they'll keep you entertained," he said as he turned and walked away.

As she watched him go, she couldn't help but think that he seemed too good to be true. She had always been such a pessimist. For once in her life, she was going to try and be optimistic. *Hopefully I won't do something to screw this up.*

She decided to get her mind off River for a moment. On top of his jacket she spotted a brochure that they were given when they first entered the aquarium. Earlier she noticed that he was flipping through it. He seemed so inquisitive. She liked that about him. As she began to flip through the brochure, she stopped on a page that had an article with a photo of a large baseball field. She couldn't help but think about River, and how hard it must have been for him that day when his dad never showed up. Skimming over the article, she read that the team was a sponsor for the aquarium. According to the article, on certain days of the year a few inner-city kids were selected to participate in a program where they are taken to the aquarium for the day and then to a baseball game at night. She continued to read on about the family that was chosen last year. One sentence caught her eye and she suddenly felt like someone dumped a bucket of cold water on her. *It's just a coincidence*, she thought to herself. *I'm not going to allow myself to have any negative thoughts. We'll probably have a laugh about it later.* She read the sentence again:

Sixty-year-old Marie Castillo of the Bronx says that she and her two grandsons, Jack, age four, and Robert, or 'Robbie' as they like to call him, age two, had a fantastic time last year when they visited the aquarium and attended the baseball game.

Chapter 5

Delilah sat on the blanket staring at the penguins. There was one penguin she couldn't seem to take her eyes off of. Even as River was talking about his family, her eyes would drift over to the little penguin. He looked smaller than the other eight or so penguins with which he shared the exhibit. What caught her attention was a large gash that ran vertically along his flipper. She also noticed that he liked to sit way up on top of a rock, away from the other penguins. Delilah wondered how he got that wound and guessed that one of the other penguins attacked him. Now it seemed like all the others have shunned him, too. *Was it because he didn't fight back?* He looked content sitting atop that rock. Perhaps he preferred being alone. If he waddled back down and tried to socialize with the other penguins again, he risked getting hurt. *Just stay where you are, little penguin.*

Be positive, Delilah thought to herself as she saw River walking back toward her. She decided not to mention anything about the family in the brochure. For now, she was just going to have to believe that it was a coincidence. She didn't think she was ready to believe anything else.

"Hey, did you miss me?" River asked as he sat back down next to her.

She decided to ignore the question. "How did your uncle say everything is going at the office?"

"Good. I'll probably go back again tomorrow."

"Are you sure that you're up to it?" she asked.

"Believe me, I'm fine," he said.

I don't know what to believe anymore. All she knew was that right now, for selfish reasons, she didn't want River going back to work. She loved spending the day with him today and, despite everything, she wanted to spend the day with him again tomorrow.

"I'm sure your uncle will like having you back. By the way, I don't think I ever asked the name of your uncle's firm."

"It's called Edwards and Carter, Attorneys at Law. The Carter is my uncle, Daniel Carter."

"Maybe you can make partner one day and your name will be up there with them," she said.

"That would be nice, but trust me, Delilah, that's not going to happen."

"Why not? You have your whole life ahead of you. You know I would really like to meet your uncle one of these days," she rambled. "I know it would be hard for me to meet your brother Josh and his family right now since they're so far away, but maybe I can come by your office one day and meet your uncle. What did you say your nephews' names were again?" she asked suspiciously.

"Jack and Robbie. Delilah, are you all right?"

"That's right. I knew I liked the names." *It's just a coincidence*, she thought. "Yes, I'm fine. Why are you asking?" *I'm always so negative, the eternal pessimist. Stop this!* She looked at River and smiled. "So are you about ready to leave?"

"Yes—not that I want to. I've had a really good time today," he said as he leaned over to kiss her cheek. Delilah didn't know what it was about him, but every time he kissed her, she could literally feel cool shivers running up and down her spine.

"You know, Delilah, I'd like to meet your family, too."

"Yes, of course," she said, a little surprised. "I would definitely like for you to meet my parents. My dad isn't living with us right now, so you would just be meeting my mother, Susan."

"Oh, I didn't know that your dad wasn't living with you."

"How could you? I never brought it up."

"I'm sorry."

"It's fine. He and my mother just started fighting a lot after—" She stopped herself realizing it was too soon to get into that. "They just needed a break from each other," she said. "I'd like for you to meet my mother. I know that as soon as she finds out about you, there will be no stopping her from meeting you."

"Well, how about today?" River asked casually.

"Today?"

"Yes. I have to drop you home anyway; why don't I come in and introduce myself?"

"Okay, I guess that will work," Delilah said, pleasantly surprised by River's confidence. In the past she dated guys who would rather cut off their right arm than meet a girl's parents. River was different. He kept surprising her. She hoped that would continue—in a good way.

When they got back to the car, Delilah called her mother to let her know that she would be bringing a guest home. She didn't want to say much in the car with River sitting right beside her, so Delilah tried to make the conversation short and sweet, completely ignoring the barrage of questions from the other end of the line. Delilah opted to just make up her own conversation. "Yes, Mom, his name is River. That's nice. I'm glad you're excited to meet him. Dinner? I'm not sure; I'll have to ask him." In reality the conversation on her mother's side was very different. Her mother was yelling in her ear, asking why this is the first time she's hearing about this guy and how could Delilah spend the whole day with a strange man that she didn't even know? Suddenly her mother hung up on her and Delilah had to keep the fake conversation going. "That sounds good, but don't go to any trouble. We could always just order Chinese. Okay, Mom, I'll see you soon." For good measure, she decided to throw in an "I love you" before ending the call.

"That's nice the way the two of you say 'I love you' before hanging up."

"Thanks, I guess it is." *If he only knew that she had already hung up.*

When they pulled up in front of Delilah's house, River commented on how nice it looked from the outside. Although Delilah knew that he was trying to be kind, the comment almost felt condescending. *Maybe I'm just sensitive*, she thought to herself. When they got to the front door, it was already open and her mother was standing behind the screen.

"Hi, Mom. This is my friend, River. River, this is my mother, Susan."

"Hi, River. It's very nice to meet you," Susan said, holding out her hand.

"It's very nice to meet you, too," River said while taking her hand and giving it a gentle shake. "I feel like Susan is too informal, maybe—"

"There's no reason to call me Mrs. Simms. We—" As she shook River's hand, a weird look crossed her face. Susan quickly pulled her hand away and cleared her throat before continuing to talk. "We, uh, aren't very formal around here, are we, D?" she said while turning to look at Delilah.

"As long as you don't mind me calling you by your first name," River said.

"Not at all. So you've been seeing each other for a couple of days already?" Susan said, quickly changing the subject. "Please come inside and have a seat," she said, directing him to the sofa. "I must admit I was a bit surprised when D said she was bringing you over."

"I'm sure you were. To be honest, I'm a bit surprised to be sitting here with you right now."

"River and I only met a few days ago, but I think it feels like a lot longer for both of us," Delilah said, touching his shoulder.

"How did the two of you meet?" Susan asked. Delilah could tell that her mother was uncomfortable. She was sitting with her legs tightly crossed, and the veins were protruding from her skinny hands as she squeezed them tightly together.

"Well—" Delilah began to speak, but River interrupted.

"Will you both excuse me for a moment? I have to use the restroom."

After River left the room, Delilah's mother turned and looked at her. "How did he know where the bathroom was?" she asked curiously.

Delilah hesitated for a moment, afraid that her mother already knew he had been in the house before. "Well, it's not like we live in a mansion, Mom. It's not very hard to find. Why are you acting so tense?"

"What do you mean?" Susan asked innocently.

"You just seem to be acting strangely," Delilah said.

"I'm not acting strangely. I think under the circumstances, I'm doing the best I can. Wait a minute," her mother put her finger to her lips and motioned for Delilah to be quiet. "Do you hear that?"

"Hear what?" Delilah asked, annoyed.

"It sounds like whispering," Susan said.

"I don't hear anything. Mom, please try to relax. I'm sorry that I didn't tell you about him sooner, but everything has just happened so fast and we really haven't had time to talk."

"I know. I'm sorry. You seem happy, and if he's the reason for that, then I'm completely on board."

"Thank you."

"That is, of course, if he's treating you well. With all that you have going on, you're very vulnerable right now, and I just want to make sure that you aren't rushing into anything."

"I'm not," Delilah said, trying to reassure her.

"I think your father should meet River, too. Maybe we can all have dinner one night this week."

Susan looked so frail, so desperate. Delilah knew that she was grateful for the excuse to plan dinner with Joe. She knew how much Susan missed him. Delilah gave her a smile and reached out to touch her hand.

"Those pictures of you in the hall are really cute, D," River said as he walked back into the room.

Delilah had forgotten about all the pictures hanging on the wall from when she was little. There was still a photograph on the wall of her and Charlotte taken in Charlotte's backyard one night when they were having a campout. They had their arms around one another and they were each holding a small battery-operated lantern. They are smiling widely, exposing the holes where their front teeth used to be. They had noticed their loose teeth at the same time and decided to have a contest to see who would be the first to lose a tooth. Delilah won by three days. She gave credit to all the apples she had deliberately eaten that week.

"I like the picture of you in the pink tutu," River said.

"Delilah never took ballet. That isn't a picture of Delilah; it's her little sister, Darcy."

"Mom, I haven't told River about Darcy yet," Delilah said, wishing her mother hadn't mentioned Darcy.

"Oh, I'm sorry. I thought the subject of your sister would have come up by now," Susan said disdainfully.

"Really, mom?" Delilah couldn't believe her mother was trying to make her feel guilty. *If only she knew that all I feel is guilt, practically every day of my life, because of what happened to my sister.*

"I understand. Will you two excuse me for a moment?" Susan snapped, not waiting for an answer before hurrying from the room.

"Where is she going?" River asked as he reached for Delilah's hand.

"Probably to Darcy's old room," Delilah said. "Darcy was my little sister. She had an accident a few years ago and she passed away."

"D, I'm so sorry."

"No, I'm sorry. I should have told you about her."

"You're not the one who should apologize. I was doing all the talking. I should have asked more questions about you."

"No, I wanted to know about you. It's fine, really." In a strange way Delilah felt like River already knew her so well that she didn't need to talk about herself.

"When did you lose your sister?" River asked gently.

"To be honest, it was sort of like I lost my sister twice. She first started to slip away from us when she was around fifteen months old. We don't know what happened; even the doctors and specialists couldn't explain it. It seemed like overnight she just stopped laughing, smiling, or showing any signs of affection. It was very sad for all of us, especially my mom."

"How old were you then?"

"A little over eleven. Having been an only child for so long, I was so excited to find out that I was going to have a sibling, and then the accident happened when she was three."

They could hear Susan crying from the next room.

"My mother likes to go in my sister's room when she's upset. She wants to feel closer to Darcy. She believes that she can still communicate with her. That's kind of crazy, right?"

"How?" River asked curiously.

"How what?" Delilah asked, confused.

"How does she communicate with her?" he asked. "I mean, does she use a Ouija board or something?"

"I don't know for sure. I try not to pay too much attention to that stuff."

"When did she start?"

"What? Speaking with the dead?" Delilah said mockingly. "I guess everything started a few weeks after my sister died." She was surprised by River's interest. "Listen, I'm really sorry that I brought you here today. We were having such a great time, and now I feel like everything is ruined."

"No, nothing is ruined," River said, leaning in to give Delilah a hug. She squeezed him back tightly. Being in his arms felt so good—somehow she felt safer, more secure.

"I'm really embarrassed by my mother. She's usually not like that," Delilah said, starting to cry.

"What's the matter? Look at me." River gently put his hand under her chin and lifted her face to his, wiping away tears from her eyes with his thumbs. "There's no reason for you to feel embarrassed. Everything is going to be all right," he said as he held her in his arms.

"I'm really glad you're here," Delilah said, squeezing him harder. Suddenly she felt that same familiar shiver run up and down her spine.

The following morning Delilah woke with a smile on her face. This was the first time she felt happy in months, and she knew it was because of River. Although she would love nothing more than to relish in the moment, Delilah couldn't ignore the gnawing pang of doubt she had about what River told her about his family. Delilah considered calling his uncle's law firm anonymously, though she wanted to trust him. She needed to trust him. She wanted to tell him all about her sister's accident, but she was afraid to. How could she tell him that she's the one—the one who was responsible for her sister's death?

Chapter 6

The next morning, Delilah was awakened by the sound of her heart pounding in her ears. Her chest felt tight and she was having trouble breathing. She tried to take a deep breath, but it felt impossible. She jumped out of bed. Her body felt weak; her fingertips were numb. *Oh God! I'm having a heart attack!* She sat on the edge of her bed, closing her eyes, and trying to slowly breathe. "It's not a heart attack," she said out loud. "You've experienced this before. It's just a panic attack." *I can deal with this.* No matter how many panic attacks she's had in her life, she always thought that the current one was the one that was going to kill her. She tried to stay calm and not think about the day ahead. Today she was going back to school.

River left last night shortly after her mother had excused herself from the living room. He thought she and her mother needed some time alone. Delilah couldn't disagree. She went into Darcy's old room and found Susan sprawled out on Darcy's bed. She was sobbing, not because of Darcy, but because of Delilah. She told Delilah how sorry she was and how embarrassed she was about her behavior. Delilah tried to reassure her, telling her that it wasn't a big deal and that River enjoyed meeting her. Delilah thought it made her feel better because her mother seemed to calm down a bit. Then Susan told her how she finally had the opportunity to speak with her principal, Mr. Dreyson. He assured Susan that he would address the problems that Delilah was having at school. Unfortunately, Delilah took no comfort in this at all. She had already seen what his idea of "addressing the problem" was. Once, when she was being shoved down the hall by one of the Imitators, Mr. Dreyson calmly said, "Let's keep our hands to ourselves," as if he was reprimanding a three-year-old. He never even looked back to see if they had stopped. Delilah didn't bother trying to explain how she felt about Mr. Dreyson to her mother; she just thanked her for calling him and trying to help. She kissed her mother on the forehead and walked out of the room, leaving her lying there on Darcy's bed hugging an oversized giraffe her sister had named "Stretch." It had been her favorite.

Delilah sat on her bed thinking about the day ahead, trying hard to shake the panicky feeling that she had by taking deep breaths through her nose and exhaling slowly through her mouth. Thinking about River helped her calm herself. She was grateful that he had come into her life. Even though she'd only known him for a short time, she felt as though it had been years. Yet, there was still so much she didn't know about him. There was a part of her that was afraid to get too close for fear that she would lose him or learn something about him that she didn't want to know. For now, just thinking about him was a great distraction at times like this, when the thought of going back to school was literally taking her breath away.

She slowly stood up and walked over to her closet. She thought about what she should wear. She usually picked out dark clothes--dressing like her mother a lot these days. Her mother wore dark colors because she's still mourning Darcy. Delilah wore dark colors not only because she still mourned her sister, but because she also mourned the life she used to have. Suddenly tired again, she walked back to her bed and threw herself down face-first. Her mind wandered to the time when she first met Charlotte Moy.

Delilah met Charlotte when they were in the first grade. Charlotte had always been the most popular girl at school. Delilah thought some of her popularity had to do with the fact that her mother, Grace, was very involved in school, as well as many of the extracurricular activities. Charlotte had an older brother named Joseph and an older sister named Pamela, so by the time Charlotte came along, Grace could plan a book drive or a bake sale with her eyes closed. Grace was also friendly with a lot of the other stay-at-home mothers, and they would often organize play dates for their daughters. They never included Delilah because her mother worked and she wasn't in the "mom clique."

Delilah used to get angry with her mother for not being more involved. For a six-year-old, it was hard to understand why some moms didn't have as much time as others to be involved at school. She eventually understood that some moms worked because they wanted to, and others worked because they had to. Her mother was the latter. Delilah was sure that her mother would have liked to stay home, but they needed the extra income. Delilah never had the impression that Charlotte's family needed extra money. They lived in a beautiful house about five minutes from Delilah, and Charlotte always came to school with the nicest clothes and newest toys, which probably contributed to her popularity.

By the time they were in fourth grade, Charlotte was as popular as ever. She formed a group with six other girls, and it was obvious that Charlotte was the one everyone else aspired to be. If Charlotte came to school with a new hairstyle or a new color of nail polish, by the end of the week everyone else in the group was sporting the same look. Delilah used to try and copy her style, too—not that anyone noticed. Overall, though, they were a nice group of girls—nothing like the clique they later formed in high school.

Delilah became obsessed with the idea of being friends with Charlotte and the other girls. She didn't think it was fair that she never had the chance to be friends with them in the first place; something that made her resent her mother. Susan was only friendly with one other mother—Nora Peterson's mom, Claire. Delilah still had classes with Nora and she was just as annoying as she was in elementary school. Back when they were kids, the only play dates Susan would set up for Delilah were with Nora. Delilah assumed that everyone thought she was like Nora because they were always together. She desperately wanted to prove to everyone that she wasn't like Nora. She knew that she could prove it to them if they would just give her a chance.

To even get close to the clique, Delilah knew she first had to become friends with Charlotte. That was the key to being in her group, and that's what Delilah wanted most toward the end of fourth grade. She knew that time was running out and middle school was just around the corner—a time when a person's identity was defined, or so she thought. She wanted to start her new school with a new group of friends. Sometimes she would actually sit around and think about how to become friends with Charlotte. If she could find a way to get Charlotte alone, away from the other girls she knew she could make it happen. One day she saw her opportunity.

It was a Saturday afternoon and she was at the park with Kim Philips. Kim lived a couple of houses down from Delilah, and on occasion she would babysit Delilah.

Delilah saw Charlotte with her mother and brother. She walked over to the seesaw where Charlotte was gleefully bouncing up and down with Joseph. She stood there for a moment and watched as Charlotte's long tresses bounced each time the seesaw came down. Delilah didn't know what to say to her, so she walked back over to where Kim was watching a group of boys playing basketball. This apparently became a big distraction for the boys, because one by one, they came over to talk to her. Kim was an attractive girl and very well-endowed; at only sixteen she was at least a C-cup. Kim knew she could attract attention and encouraged it with her tight-fitting tops.

Delilah called Kim's name a few times, but she was engrossed in conversation with an emaciated-looking blonde boy wearing a baseball cap turned backwards. Delilah knew that Kim regretted having her along. She overheard Kim say to the boy, "I'm just babysitting to earn some extra cash. I really wish I didn't have to. Maybe I can meet a nice guy who will take me out." Kim stroked her chestnut hair for emphasis. Delilah had to say one thing for Kim—she wasn't subtle.

To be honest, Delilah did know that Kim secretly liked spending time with her, but on that day it was apparently more important for her to try to sound cool in front of malnourished-looking adolescents. Regardless, Delilah was still mad at her for making the comment, and she quickly came up with a plan. She managed to make herself appear weepy by pulling out a couple of nose hairs with her fingernail. Then she ran over to Grace, who was dutifully watching her own children play. With her red and watering eyes, Delilah knew that Grace would take pity on her. She was just the type who thrived on helping out a kid in need, although it wasn't always clear what she liked more: helping a child or telling everyone that she had. Delilah could still remember the concerned look on her face when she saw her.

"What's the matter, dear?" Grace asked.

"My babysitter left me here," Delilah sobbed. "She started talking to some of her friends, and then she just took off with them."

"That's terrible, Denise."

"My name's Delilah." She had been in her daughter's class for four years and Grace still didn't know her name.

"Well, Delilah," she said repeating her name, "you can come home with us and I'll contact your mother. Imagine leaving a child alone in a park. That girl should be whipped." Charlotte's mother was always very dramatic. She was raised in the south and had an accent, which to Delilah made everything she said sound theatrical.

When they got back to Charlotte's house, Grace told them to go upstairs and play while she called Delilah's mother. As Delilah walked up the stairs and into Charlotte's perfectly pink room—complete with a beaded chandelier and canopy bed—she forgot all about Kim, who was probably out of her mind with worry. Thinking back now, she couldn't believe how excited she had been to be in Charlotte's room.

"Are you okay?" Charlotte asked. She spoke with a trace of a southern accent herself. "I can't believe your sitter just ditched you," she said sympathetically.

"I know, and she was always so cool," Delilah said, almost starting to believe her own lie.

"Delilah, dear, I'm not getting any answer over at your house," Grace said, poking her head around the door. "I'll keep trying until I reach her." She tried to sound reassuring. "I'll make you girls some popcorn and hot chocolate while you wait. How does that sound?" she asked as she walked away, not waiting for a reply. Delilah prayed that Charlotte's mother reached her mom before Kim did. She could only imagine the look on her mother's face when Kim broke the news that she had lost her daughter in the park. Suddenly, Delilah began to feel very guilty.

"Do you want to give each other makeovers?" Charlotte asked.

"Sure," Delilah replied, immediately forgetting her guilt.

Charlotte's mother popped back into the room a little while later, holding a tray with two steaming mugs of hot chocolate and a big bowl of popcorn. She laughed when she saw Charlotte and Delilah with their hair in rollers and their faces covered in makeup.

"Oh my goodness, just look at the two of you!" she exclaimed. "Delilah, dear, we'd better make sure you wash all that gunk off your face before your mother sees you. I left her a message telling her that you're at our house, so I'm sure she'll be calling here any minute."

Charlotte and Delilah carried on playing while they waited for Susan to call. Delilah thought Charlotte was probably surprised at how well they hit it off, but Delilah wasn't. She always knew that she and Charlotte could be really good friends. Just as they were about to start a game of Go Fish, they heard the doorbell ring. It was Susan, and she wasn't happy.

"Delilah, would you please explain to me exactly what happened?" She sounded completely frantic. "I just can't believe that Kim could do something like this. I mean, her mother told me that she could sometimes be a bit irresponsible, but I never thought that she was capable—"

"Mom, please calm down. We just got separated, that's all."

"Oh, is that all?" Susan said facetiously. "If it hadn't been for Mrs. Moy, you would still be alone in the park with God-only-knows-who." She turned to Grace and thanked her profusely for helping. Grace kept saying that there was no need to thank her and that she would be sure to spread the word to the other moms about Kim's irresponsible behavior. With all the mothers Charlotte's mom knew, Delilah realized right then and there that Kim's babysitting days were over. She began to feel the guilt creep back up inside of her.

"Hey, Delilah, maybe we can sit together tomorrow at lunch," Charlotte shouted from the stairs—and just like that her guilt subsided again. She knew it was a rotten thing to do to Kim, but she also knew that Kim would be fine; even if she wasn't, a small part of Delilah didn't care. She had gotten what she wanted.

If she had only known then what she knew now--Susan never spoke to Kim or her mother again after that day. Kim went home and told her mother her version of the story, the truth. Susan didn't want to hear that Delilah had just wandered off. She thought Kim should have been paying attention to Delilah, not a group of boys.

Years later, Delilah saw Kim and her mother at Darcy's wake. All things considered, it was nice of them to have come. Delilah glanced over at Kim, who was wearing a tight fitting top that exposed her ample breasts. They looked as if they had grown two more cup sizes since she had seen her last. They never said a word to Delilah or her family; they just paid their respects and left. Delilah sat through the rest of the service resting her head on Charlotte's shoulder. Charlotte stroked her hair and comforted her as she cried.

Charlotte and Delilah became the best of friends, but they were always part of a larger group. Through the years, though, they remained the only two constants in the group. In middle school there were six of them, but only one of the other girls was from the original set. No matter how much their friends changed, one thing stayed the same: Delilah and Charlotte were the ones everyone else wanted to be with. Delilah was able to recognize the desperate look on the other girls' faces when they tried to sit with the popular pair at lunch — she used to be one of them. Delilah always tried to be nice and would move over to make room for the hopefuls, but she felt sorry for them. She knew that their efforts were in vain and that they would never really fit in with the clique.

By the time they started high school three years later, it was just Charlotte and Delilah. Two of the girls in their group had moved, and a couple of others had gone on to parochial school. Delilah knew that this scared Charlotte to death, but she also knew that Charlotte would figure out a way to become one of the most popular girls in high school — no matter what the cost.

Charlotte's brother, Joseph, started dating Rachael Nappi only after Charlotte arranged it.

Rachael went to a different middle school, but it fed into the same high school as Delilah and Charlotte. Everyone knew that Rachael was very popular in middle school, especially Charlotte, who became fast friends with her as soon as Joseph and Rachael started dating. By association, Delilah also became one of Rachael's friends, but there was something about her that Delilah disliked immediately. By the time school started in September, they had already formed their new clique: Delilah, Charlotte, Rachael, and two of Rachael's friends, Emily and Natalie. It was strange to Delilah how they all hung out together right from the start, as if they'd known each other all their lives.

Delilah looked over at the clock and she saw that it was already quarter to eight. She knew she needed to get moving if she is going to make it to school on time. She took a fast shower and slicked her hair back into a ponytail while it was still wet. She picked out a pair of black sweats and a gray fitted tee. It helped her to dress more comfortably these days, considering how far she had to walk when she got off the bus. She tried to choke down some corn flakes, but started to feel like she was going to throw up, so she decided to drink a glass of orange juice instead. She tied on her Nikes with the pink swoosh, grabbed a sweatshirt, her backpack, and keys, and ran out the front door.

As she entered the school building, things seemed eerily quiet. She was a few minutes late, so she had to stop at the main office to get a late pass. As she waited, she could hear the secretary behind the counter on the phone with what sounded like a disgruntled parent.

"No, there is nothing I can do to speed up the principal's meeting. I'm afraid you're just going to have to wait for it to end to discuss your son's progress — or lack thereof — in science." The secretary rolled her eyes and held up her index finger to Delilah, indicating that she will only be another minute. "Yes, I will be sure to have him call you just as soon as he's through. Thank you." She hung up the phone. "Wow, they really come out of the woodwork sometimes," she said to Delilah with a snort. "Now, I'm guessing you need a late pass, am I right?"

"Yes, please," Delilah said. As the secretary began to fill out her pass, the phone rang again. She picked it up and held the phone with her shoulder. Delilah remembered her mom's chiropractor saying that was one of the worst things you could do to your neck.

"James Madison High, how can I help you?" The secretary handed Delilah the pass and smiled. As Delilah turned to walk away, she saw two young girls who looked like freshmen staring at her. She couldn't help but wonder if they might have heard an untrue rumor about her.

As she walked to class, she looked down at her pass and realized that the secretary forgot to write the time. Deciding to take advantage of the situation, she slowly removed some items from her locker, and walked down to the bathroom. She opened the door to all three stalls and scanned the walls with her eyes to see if anything new had been written about her. The coast seemed clear. Resting her backpack on the radiator, she walked over to the sink and looked in the mirror. She looked like hell. Turning on the faucet, she splashed some cold water on her face. When she looked up, she was startled by another face staring back at her in the mirror. It was Nora Peterson.

Nora took secret pleasure in the fall of Delilah's popularity, but because their mothers were such good friends, Nora had to pretend like she cared. Meanwhile, Delilah knew that Nora would give her mother's right arm to hang with the Imitators even for a day, but that would never happen.

Nora was an old soul and seemed to enjoy spending time with her mother's friends. Susan always said that she wished Delilah enjoyed spending time with her the way Nora enjoyed spending time with Claire.

"Hey, Delilah. I haven't seen you around school in a while. Where have you been?"

"I was a little under the weather the past couple of days, so I decided to stay home and rest."

"Well, I hope you're feeling better," Nora said, sounding skeptical.

"I am. Thanks for asking. Okay, well, I guess I'll see you around," Delilah said as she tried to walk back to class.

"Okay—oh, and by the way, I don't know if your mom mentioned it to you or not, but my mom and I are going to be coming to your house this Saturday night."

"Oh, that's nice. Maybe we can catch a movie or something," Delilah said, trying to be friendly.

"No can do," Nora giggled. "I'm really looking forward to what your mother has planned for us."

"What does my mother have planned?"

"Oh, she hasn't told you? Well, maybe you should hear it from her."

"Hear what from her?" Delilah said, annoyed.

"The séance," Nora said, like it was the most normal thing in the world.

"Séance?" Delilah repeated, hoping that she misunderstood.

"Yes. Surely you know that your mother has wanted to do this for a while now, and she finally decided on this weekend," Nora said excitedly.

Delilah shook her head, as if she had heard all of this before. She decided not to let Nora know that she was completely in the dark about the whole thing. Although she had to admit, she really wasn't in the dark. Her mother had tried to talk to her about the many books she had read on the topic of life after death. She even told Delilah how she still saw and communicated with Darcy in their house. Thinking about it now, Delilah felt bad because she had never taken anything her mother has said on the topic seriously. In fact, she usually just ignored her; always assuming that her mother just needed a way to deal with her grief. Delilah never wanted to appear condescending by telling her mother how wonderful she thought it was that she communicated with her dead sister. In reality, she thought that her mother's behavior was unhealthy and that she needed to move on. Her mother must have sensed her trepidation, because she never once mentioned anything to Delilah about the séance. Even with everything she's done so far, Delilah never thought she would do something as twisted as this.

"You know what, Nora, my mom and I have different beliefs about this sort of thing. I don't think I'll be participating in any séance."

"Oh, come on," Nora said snarkily. "I've heard stories about you and your former friends tilting a table or two."

Wow, I guess all girls can be bitchy. She couldn't believe that Nora brought that up. A while back, Charlotte and Delilah went down to Rachael's basement with the rest of the girls because Rachael had read somewhere about table tilting, an odd practice used to conjure spirits. Apparently when the alphabet was recited, the table was supposed to tilt when certain letters were called, thus spelling out words and sentences coming from the deceased—similar to using a Ouija board. Rachael was obsessed with the idea of contacting her grandmother. The two of them had been very close when she was growing up.

"Really, Nora? Did my mother tell your mom about that?"

"Yes, she did!" Nora said defiantly. "So don't stand there and pretend that you're better than me—"

"What?" Delilah said, cutting her off midsentence. "What are you talking about?"
Apparently this girl has some unresolved issues with me.

"Well, it's just that I know you've always thought you were better than me," Nora squawks, pushing her glasses up on her nose.

"Nora, that's not true," Delilah protested. *Why is it that everyone in my life wants to argue with me?* Delilah couldn't believe how some people knew just how to attack when a person was their most vulnerable. It was such animalistic behavior. She never thought Nora had the nerve to speak to anyone like this. Actually, Delilah knew that Nora wouldn't be speaking to her like this if she weren't aware of her situation with the Imitators.

"Do you remember how I used to sit there in your house, while you were getting ready to go out? You never once asked if I would like to hang out with you and your friends."

"Nora, you're not being fair. You never acted like you wanted to come with me. I thought you liked staying with your mom and my mom." Delilah felt weird saying that. Hearing it out loud, she supposed no one would believe that. Maybe she made herself believe it because she no longer wanted to be associated with Nora like she had been in elementary school.

"Believe whatever you want. I'm really over it," Nora said, but her manner belied her words. "My point is that I've heard stories about how you and your little posse used to table tilt. You used to have your satanic rituals to try and awaken the dead, and now you're going to turn up your nose at something that isn't half as bad. Your mom is doing this with us because she has no one else to turn to. She feels like she's going crazy because no one believes her. I mean, it's obvious you have no interest in what she says."

"You don't know anything about my relationship with my mother," Delilah said, on the verge of tears.

"I know more than you think. She talks to my mother all the time. So believe me when I tell you that she is completely frustrated over the fact that everyone is making her feel like she's crazy. Even your dad moved out and left her."

"How dare you speak about my father," Delilah snapped, trying to control her rage.

"I'm just trying to help you understand your mother so maybe you can be a little more empathetic."

"I can't believe that you're going to stand there and tell me about my mother. Who do you think you are?"

"Oh, that's right, how dare I speak my mind to the great Delilah," Nora said sarcastically. "I hate to break it to you, D, but you're just like me now. You've fallen off your high horse."

"And I bet you're loving every second of it. I have to say, you really had me fooled. I never thought you were this malicious. I always had my suspicions that you envied me, but this—this is just pathetic."

"I don't envy you. I would never want to be in your situation."

"Believe me, Nora, you would never *be* in my situation. You would have to have friends first in order to lose them." Nora stared at Delilah, stunned, like a deer caught in headlights. Remorse crashed over Delilah.

"Nora, I'm sorry. It's just that when you mentioned my father I—"

"Please don't bother saying anything else."

"It just seems that you have some built-up resentment for something that I never intentionally did. Listen, I don't want things to be awkward every time we see each other. We should at least pretend to get along, since our mothers are such good friends."

"I agree. And I will be at your house this weekend, whether or not you wish to participate."

"Nora, you do realize that you're talking about my little sister, right? This may seem like your idea of a fun-filled Saturday night, but conjuring up the spirit of my deceased sister really makes me uncomfortable."

"I'm sorry. I guess I was being a little insensitive. I just assumed that you were on the same page as your mom with this whole thing. The idea of it excites her. To be honest, it excites me, too. I'm hoping my grandfather comes through. I never had the chance to tell him how much I loved him."

"Well, maybe you'll get your chance on Saturday," Delilah said.

"Maybe," Nora said. "Look, I have to get to class. I'll see you later."

"Later," Delilah said with a weak attempt at a wave.

Delilah felt like the conversation she just had with Nora was surreal. Of all the horrible things she was expecting to happen today, having an argument with Nora and finding out her mother was planning a séance with the neighbors was not one of them. She felt like she needed to get out of the building and talk to someone. She wanted River. His lucid point of view on things would really help right now. She knew that if he was with her, he would find a way to make her feel better, "You're a lot stronger than you think." River's words echoed in her head. She knew that she had to get her act together and get herself to homeroom, which was just about to end.

After the long walk down the corridor, she stood outside her homeroom door. Her heart was pounding out of her chest. She needed to calm down. The day has just started and she was already feeling completely stressed out. Taking a deep breath, she opened the door. It felt like every eye in the class was boring into her flesh. She quickly took her seat at the back of the room and removed the late pass from her pocket, checked the time and quickly wrote it in on the line, trying to disguise her handwriting.

"Miss Simms, do you have something for me?" Ms. Cooper, the homeroom teacher, asked condescendingly. *Why does she have to be so patronizing? Why can't she just come out and ask me for my late pass?*

"Yes, Ms. Cooper, I have it right here," Delilah said walking up the middle aisle. She glanced at Charlotte, but her face was buried in a book. If it were any of the other Imitators sitting there, Delilah would have to watch her step; they were notorious for sticking out their foot to try and trip her. Charlotte had never tried that. Her relationship with Charlotte was really odd; Charlotte was definitely an Imitator, and as the name implied, she pretty much did whatever the rest of the girls did — except when it came to Delilah. She almost seemed to keep out of it. Delilah tried to get her alone to talk a few times, but Charlotte never said anything. Charlotte had always been popular, and the thought of not being popular terrified her.

Delilah got back to her seat just as the third bell rang. Everyone, including Charlotte, jumped up and ran for the door. Delilah followed slowly behind. She saw Rachael Nappi and Emily Baxter waiting in the hall for Charlotte. As she walked past, they started in on her again.

"Look who decided to grace us with her presence today! We were hoping that you would never come back," Rachael Nappi said with a devious smile.

"Be honest, Rae, we would really miss not having our little Delilah to push around," Emily said.

"I guess you're right, Em. What do you think, Char?" Rachael turned to Charlotte.

"I really think I better get to class before Mr. Smith has my ass. I'll see you guys later." Charlotte walked away and doesn't look back.

Delilah briskly walked by Emily and Rachael. She knew that they also had their first class on the third floor. She decided to go up the staircase marked "down," hoping to avoid them.

"Are you trying to lose us, bitch? Why do you even bother coming back to school? You know no one wants you here," Rachael said, snapping her gum. She continued to walk up the stairs.

"If I were you, I would just kill myself," Emily said. Delilah felt her blood begin to boil. She thought about how she smashed that guy in the face with a brick at the park, and quickly tried to muster that same courage.

"That's a good idea. Why don't you pretend that you're me and just kill *yourself*?" As Delilah heard the words coming out of her mouth, she couldn't believe she was saying them. She had never said anything back to her tormenters before. She always thought that it would only make them angrier. She hoped that someday they would feel sorry for her and just give up. Obviously she was giving them way too much credit. It felt good to actually stand up for herself, and the look on Rachael's face was well worth any retaliation she might have coming.

"You little bitch! Who do you think you're talking to? I am going to rip every hair out of your head."

Delilah walked away, not looking back. Suddenly, she heard Mr. Dreyson, the principal. He was a small man whose receding hairline and potbelly made him look like a weasel.

"Is there a problem here ladies?" Mr. Dreyson asked Rachael and Emily.

"We don't have a problem," Rachael glowered.

"Well, I noticed the two of you are using the down staircase to go up. I can give you detention for that, you know."

Is this guy for real? Delilah thought to herself. Even after her mother spoke to him, he's going to threaten detention for using the wrong staircase? How about giving detention for making threats on people's lives? She decided to sneak ahead before he gave her detention, too. As she slipped through the door, she could hear Rachael shriek with indignation.

"What about her? She was using the wrong staircase, too!" Delilah just kept walking, but Mr. Dreyson never called her back. She wondered if he gave Rachael and Emily detention. *If he did, it isn't doing me any favors. It will make them more mad, which will only hurt me in the end.*

Delilah walked into her first class of the day, English Literature, and smiled at her teacher, Mrs. Faulkner—no relation to the great American writer William Faulkner, or at least that's what she told the class on the first day of school. This was the second time Delilah had Mrs. Faulkner for an English class. The first time was her sophomore year. They read *Of Mice and Men* by John Steinbeck. Mrs. Faulkner assigned the class a few pages to read at home each night. She would never tell the students to read more than a few pages unless they wanted to. She believed that the quantity of pages read didn't matter and that students should be encouraged to read because it's enjoyable, not to complete an assignment.

Mrs. Faulkner was also the first and only teacher to acknowledge Delilah's problems at school. One day during the first week of school, Mrs. Faulkner knelt down beside Delilah while she was doing her work and whispered that she would like to see her after class. She told Delilah that she noticed some of the things that were going on at school. Even though Delilah assured her that she was okay, she could tell the teacher felt bad for her. Mrs. Faulkner tried to comfort Delilah by sharing a story about how she dealt with a bully when she was in high school. Delilah didn't want to hurt her feelings by telling her that she may as well have been born with the dinosaurs because things had changed so much since Mrs. Faulkner's high school days. She didn't have to worry about social media back then and all of her business being posted on the Internet for the world to see. *People don't even have to know you or live anywhere near you to know what's going on with you nowadays.* Delilah had thought. *They can literally be anywhere in the world — even whale-watching in the Artic — and know that Rachael Nappi thinks the shirt I'm wearing today is ugly.* Nevertheless, she really did appreciate the fact that Mrs. Faulkner took the time to try to help her, and she knew that even after she graduated, she would never forget her English Lit teacher.

Mrs. Faulkner smiled from across the classroom and mouthed to Delilah, "Are you all right?" She could probably tell from Delilah's expression that her day wasn't going so well. Delilah mouthed back to her that she was fine and continued to work on the assignment that was written on the board. Delilah looked around the classroom and noticed that there's a scattering of students blankly staring at her. She couldn't believe how alone she felt. Even as she tried to concentrate on her work, her mind kept thinking about River. She couldn't wait to see him after school today. For the first time in a while, she felt like she had something to look forward to.

It was a beautiful day—it was just starting to feel like fall. Fall had always been Delilah's favorite season. She had always thought one of the nicest things about living in New York was the chance to experience all four seasons. Winter was cold and snowy, summer was hot and muggy, spring was warm, and fall was cool—just the way nature intended it to be. When she was a kid her dad used to talk about moving down south to Florida, but her mother wouldn't agree to it. Delilah couldn't help but think that her sister might still be alive if they would have bought a house, any house, in Florida.

As she thought of her sister, the wind kicked up and she felt a chill run up and down her spine. *I'm almost home – I can see the overpass now. When I get home, I will call River.* She closed her eyes and felt the wind on her face. Another chill ran up her spine. It reminded her of kissing him.

As soon as she got home, she dropped her backpack on the floor and tossed her jacket over the arm of the couch. She ran to her room and closed her bedroom door, even though no one else was home. She grabbed the phone and dialed River's cell. With any other guy she would wait at least an hour to call, making it look like she wasn't too anxious, but with River she didn't care. She wanted him to know how much she had been looking forward to hearing his voice. As she dialed his cell, butterflies rose in her stomach.

"Hey, you!" The sound of River's voice was so comforting. "I've been looking forward to hearing your voice all day," he said.

"Me too."

"So, am I going to get to see you today?" he asked.

"I hope so. What time can you leave?"

"I can probably get out of here in less than an hour. It's really quiet today."

"It sounds quiet," she said. "It doesn't even sound like there's anyone there."

"I'm in one of the conference rooms."

"Do you want to pick me up at my house, and maybe we can catch an early dinner together?" Delilah suggested.

"That sounds good. I'll pick you up at around quarter to five. Is that okay?"

"That's perfect. I'll see you later." As she hung up the phone, a strange feeling came over her. Something was nagging at her--it didn't even seem like he was in an office. A busy law firm would have some background noise. It sounded like he was calling from a closet—quiet and kind of muffled. *I'm sure he was in a conference room like he said.* Still, she couldn't shake her doubts. She decided to pick up the phone and dial information.

"I need the number for Edwards and Carter, Attorneys at Law. They're located in Manhattan." Her voice was shaky.

"Please hold for the number."

She pressed the button to be connected directly, holding the phone with baited breath. *What the hell am I doing? What if River answers the phone? What am I going to say?* She was just about to hang up when she heard a frail-sounding voice.

"Edwards and Carter, Attorneys at Law, how may I help you? Hello? Is anyone there?" the voice asked.

"H … Hello. I'm looking for River."

"River? Speak up, dear, I can't hear you."

"Yes, River Spencer. He's the nephew of Daniel Carter, right?" she asked.

"Yes … who is this?"

"I'm just a friend," she said.

"I'll direct your call to Mr. Carter. I'm sure he will want to help you."

"No, that won't be necessary," Delilah said as she hung up the phone, relieved.

Forty miles from where Delilah placed the call, at the Edwards and Carter law firm, a feeble-looking woman dialed the extension of her boss, Daniel Carter.

"Yes, Mrs. White?"

"I'm sorry to interrupt you, but I just got a strange call from a young woman who was asking for your nephew, River."

"Did she give her name?"

"No, sir, she wouldn't give her name, and there was nothing on our caller ID."

"What did you tell her?"

"Don't worry, sir. I didn't say anything."

"If she calls back again please be sure to put her through to me. I hope this isn't something I'm going to have to contact his father about. You know how sometimes these crazy people come out of the woodwork when they read a story in the paper."

"I know what you mean, sir. There are some real wackos out there, but then again, maybe it was innocent and she didn't hear about the case in the paper."

"Perhaps. By the way, Mrs. White, I'm going to need you to cancel my twelve o'clock lunch for tomorrow."

"I'll mark your calendar right now, Mr. Carter."

"What would I do without you, Mrs. White?" Daniel Carter hung up the phone, removed his glasses, closed his eyes, and squeezed the bridge of his nose. After a few seconds, he pushed back on his leather wing-back chair and looked around his office as if it were the first time he was seeing it. Sometimes he had to pinch himself to make sure it was real; he had achieved the American dream.

Daniel Carter made partner in his law firm two years ago, and last year he purchased a beautiful apartment on Park Avenue. What he was most proud of was how he was able to accomplish so much coming from so little. Despite his accomplishments, however, his heart still ached for his sister, Beth. She wasn't as fortunate as he was, and she wasn't able to escape the life they were born into. Beth became addicted to drugs and alcohol when she was just a teenager. When Daniel was offered a job at a New York City law firm, he asked her to move to New York with him, but she refused. Feeling guilty, he left and told her that he would visit whenever he was able.

A few months after moving to New York, Daniel met another young lawyer named Robert Spencer. Robert allowed Daniel to stay with him and his wife for a few months until Daniel could save enough money to get on his feet. Robert was married to his high school sweetheart; they didn't have any children. The three got along well, and the arrangement seemed to work out fine.

Daniel and Robert became very close friends, and when Daniel went to Florida one weekend to visit Beth, Robert went with him. Robert's wife was working at the time, so she couldn't join them. When Daniel introduced Robert to Beth, she was working in a dive bar. What happened between the two of them was something Daniel never would have expected. Although his sister was extremely attractive and could be very alluring at times, he never thought Robert would stray from his wife. Living with the Spencers, Daniel saw first-hand what a close bond they seemed to have, and he always envied their relationship.

On the night before Daniel and Robert were supposed to leave, they all had a little too much to drink. Daniel ended up going home with an intoxicated blonde who had spent most of the night dancing on the bar. He left Robert at the bar alone with Beth, who poured shots down his throat for the rest of the night. Daniel didn't find out that they had had an affair until two months later when his sister called to say she was pregnant. Daniel knew Beth couldn't handle another child. She already had an older son, Josh, whom she conceived during another one-night stand. Luckily for Josh, his paternal grandparents stepped in and took custody.

For some reason though, Daniel had a good feeling about this pregnancy. He convinced her to keep the baby and use it as an excuse to get herself clean and sober. She did. Daniel couldn't believe the turnaround in his sister when he went to visit her after River was born.

It wasn't until River was a little over a year old that she started using again. Daniel knew Beth wasn't happy. She tried getting along on her own, but every time Robert came to visit, she wanted him more and more for herself. She knew she would never have him, and she envied his wife in New York. A part of Daniel resented Robert for the type of relationship that he had with his sister, but he couldn't deny the fact that he was a good father to River. He even purchased a condo in Florida so he could be close to him when he visited. Since it was only a two-hour plane ride from New York, he would visit whenever he was able. Daniel knew that the connection Robert had with River only made things harder on his sister. She was miserable, and she was spiraling out of control. The one thing that seemed to keep her from completely going over the edge was the love she had for River.

As Daniel Carter sat in his office, looking out the oversized windows, he still couldn't believe that it was River who ultimately killed her.

Chapter 7

The doorbell rang while Delilah was applying her lipstick. She ran her fingers through her hair and gave herself one final glance before running to the front door. When she opened it, River was standing there with a smile that spread from ear to ear. He looked genuinely happy to see her.

"Hi," she said, trying to contain her excitement. Without saying a word, River bent down and gently kissed her lips. She felt a cool shiver run from the tips of her toes to the top of her head.

"I've missed you," he said.

"I've missed you, too," she said taking him by the hand. "Do you want to hang out here for a while? My mom won't be home for a few hours."

"No, let's go out. It's a beautiful day," he said. "Do you know a place where we can eat outside? Although, you may have to bring a sweater."

"I know just the place. I'll tell you how to get there."

Delilah directed River to the Crabby Shack. It was about fifteen minutes from her house. It looked like a hole-in-the-wall from the outside, but it had a large deck in the back with plenty of outdoor seating overlooking a beautiful pond.

"This looks like an interesting place," River said, lifting his brow.

"Just wait until you get inside. It looks a lot better—oh, excuse me." A man walked past Delilah with a little boy, who was leading two small dogs on a leash. The dogs were barking and acting excited. "Hi there, little guys," Delilah said as she bent down to pet them. One of the dogs started to growl, and Delilah quickly pulled her hand away.

"I'm sorry about that, miss," the owner of the dogs apologized. "They are usually very friendly with strangers."

"It's my fault. I probably just startled them. Have a nice day!" Delilah said as they continue to walk past.

"And that's why I'm more of a cat person, myself," River whispered to Delilah.

When they first entered the restaurant, it truly did look like a hole-in-the-wall, but past the bar there was an exit that led to the deck with a view of the pond.

"This is a hidden treasure," River said as the hostess seated them on the edge of the deck, next to the water.

"Only the locals know about it," Delilah said with a smile. "The food is really good, too. If you like seafood, they have really delicious shellfish."

"I hope they don't get it from the pond," River looked at her skeptically for a moment before his expression softened into a beautiful smile. "Just kidding."

"I know. But if you do want something from the pond, you should order the fried frog legs — they're amazing!"

"What?"

"Kidding."

"I think I'll just stick with a burger. I used to love bacon burgers."

"Did you become a vegetarian or something?"

"No, why?"

"You said that you *used* to like them."

"Yes, I just stopped eating them because there's so much saturated fat."

"But they're so good! In fact, I think I'll have the bacon cheeseburger — rare!"

"Wow, I'm very impressed. I like a girl who isn't afraid to eat meat. It's always been a turn-off when a girl orders a salad," River said, causing Delilah to laugh. "Why are you laughing?"

Before she had a chance to answer, the waitress interrupted them. River ordered a buffalo chicken sandwich and Delilah ordered a bacon cheeseburger — mooing.

"So, tell me, why were you laughing about girls who order salads on dates?"

"It's just that a lot of my old friends used to do that. They swore that girls who ate a lot turned off guys. One time, my friend Charlotte almost fainted on a date because she was so hungry. She just sat there and watched as her date scarfed down three slices of pizza. She said she went home that night and raided her fridge. When Charlotte told me that story we laughed so hard our stomachs hurt." Suddenly Delilah felt very sad, as though she had just shared a story about someone who died. As soon as it occurred to her that her face might be reflecting what she was feeling, River's expression confirmed it.

"What's wrong?"

"What do you mean?" She decided to play stupid.

"You seem upset all of a sudden," River said, concerned.

"It's nothing. I just have a lot on my mind." *Like how I only have memories of having friends, and how my mother plans on conjuring up my dead sister this weekend.*

"Listen, I told you that I want to be here for you. If you need to talk, talk to me."

Delilah sat there for a moment and looked at River. He was gazing back at her intently. In the sunlight his blue eyes looked almost transparent. She had never noticed that before. She knew she was staring and tried to look away, but she couldn't; his eyes were hypnotic.

His voice snapped her out of it. "Delilah, are you all right?"

"Yes, I'm all right. I wanted to tell you about some of the things I've been having a hard time with." She didn't know what had come over her, but she wanted to tell him everything — all the things she had been feeling, all her emotions.

"The girl, Charlotte, that I just told you about," she began.

"Yes, what about her?" River asked.

"She used to be my best friend."

"What happened?"

"We wanted to be popular when we started high school, so basically we sold ourselves to the devil."

"The devil?" River repeated, seemingly intrigued.

"Well, that's how I like to refer to her, but her real name is Rachael. When Charlotte and I started high school together, we were the only two left from our original group of friends, and that made

Charlotte nervous. She was always used to being part of a large group of girls. Girls who, for the most part, idolized her."

"Including you?" River asked innocently.

"Yes. But later, as we became closer, I think she started to admire me. I became more confident, and I didn't really care about gaining the approval of others as much as she did. Her insecurities were partly why we befriended Rachael. Charlotte and I had heard about Rachael and her friends and we knew that they didn't have a very good reputation."

"What do you mean?"

"Well, I should say they didn't have a great reputation with adults. They were always starting trouble and fighting. I also overheard some adults refer to them as tramps. At the time I didn't believe it, but I came to find out later that it was true. Charlotte knew that they would be attending the same high school as us and she convinced me that we needed to become friends with them. She said if we didn't, we risked the chance of being shunned by them, and I knew how much it meant for Charlotte to be popular. Charlotte was actually able to bribe her brother, who's three years older than her, to hook up with Rachael. I think what convinced him to do it was that he heard Rachael was easy. Apparently, he must have liked her because he stayed with her for almost a year. That was how Charlotte became part of their group—and by association, so did I."

A tall, thin waitress interrupted Delilah. "I have one bacon cheeseburger, *mooing,* for the lady," she said as she put a chipped plate down in front of Delilah. "And one buffalo chicken for the gentleman. If you need anything else, just holler."

"Everything looks good," River said before taking a bite of his sandwich. "Please continue your story."

"I'm sorry. I don't want to bore you with all of this."

"Not at all. It's obvious that something has really been upsetting you, and I want to know all about it." The look on his face seemed so genuine. She wanted to tell him everything. She took a bite of a fry, and wiped her hands on her pants. After a deep breath she continued.

"Once we became friends with Rachael, I knew it was a mistake. I tried to convince Charlotte that we didn't need her; that we could make other friends, but Charlotte refused to stop hanging out with them. I never realized just how insecure she was until I saw how much she relied on being in a group. The sad part was I knew, or I should say I know now that she didn't really like Rachael. I think she was, and still is, afraid of her."

"So what happened?" Did you decide to stop being friends with them?"

"Well, yes and no. Rachael and the rest of her little cronies made the decision for me. They methodically worked to turn Charlotte against me. They knew I never really liked them, and they didn't like how I often went against them."

"How did you go against them?" River asked.

"When didn't I go against them should be the question. I don't know," Delilah gave a long sigh and looked up at the sky. "I always thought I was doing the right thing. Like the times when they would walk around the halls and mock other students, or stay out all night without calling their parents, or sleep around with guys." She looked up at River to see his expression. He gave a little smirk and looked down at his plate. "I never did those things, and it's not like I was afraid of some type of divine intervention. I just knew that it wasn't right. I wouldn't want to intentionally hurt someone's feelings or make my parents worry about me."

"Or sleep around with losers," River added.

"Yes," Delilah said with a smile. "I just never wanted to do those things and now ... maybe I should have, because I would be a hell of a lot happier than I am right now."

"How can you say that?" River asked. "You should be proud of yourself for standing up for what you believe in. Listen to me. High school is such a small part of your life. You're going to be finished in just a few months, and this will all be a memory. Your self-worth is something you'll have forever. You didn't sell out to those girls. You should be proud of yourself for that, and as far as any divine intervention goes, believe me, there will be a time when you will be rewarded."

"What do you mean? Like in heaven?" she asked, clearly confused.

"Something like that," River said with a smile. "You can't let these girls get the better of you."

"Well, that's just it. It's not only the girls in the group. It seems to be everyone at school now."

"What happened?"

"The group, the Imitators, they set me up."

"How?"

"They set me up to make it look like I was fooling around with Charlotte's boyfriend at the time—Steve."

"What did they do?"

"They started trouble between Charlotte and Steve, then they asked me to be somewhere at a certain time—just as Steve, vulnerable and pathetic, showed up. I found out later that they told him I wanted to be with him and that I was willing to give up my friendship with Charlotte to do it.

Apparently he had always had a little thing for me, which I found out the hard way."

"What did he do?" River seemed jealous.

"He grabbed me and tried to kiss me, and it was no coincidence that Charlotte happened to walk in with Rachael at the exact moment he threw his arms around me. I'll never forget the looks on Charlotte's and Rachael's faces when they walked in. That was the moment Rachael knew she had won and my life would never be the same again. She just stood there and hugged Charlotte. The next day at school everyone was talking about it, but of course the story grew to be a hundred times worse. By the end of the day everyone was talking about how Charlotte walked in on Steve and me in bed."

"Why do you think everyone got involved?"

"Because most people thrive on other people's misery. Have you ever noticed that? Everyone denies it, but it's almost always true. A true friend is very hard to find. That's what I thought I had found in Charlotte, but she never even gave me a chance to explain. It was all anyone talked about at school for months. If Rachael doesn't like someone, everyone else jumps on the bandwagon and dislikes that person, too. It's really pathetic how something like that can make people feel validated."

"You know, that's what most people want out of life—just to feel validated. They just want to know that someone is listening to them. I think that's why social media has blown up the way it has. Some people really believe that other people care that they're eating tuna salad for lunch." River said, laughing.

"Or that we give a crap that they hate Monday mornings," Delilah added. "Do you know that it took less than twenty-four hours for Photoshopped pictures of me and Steve in bed to appear? People were saying really derogatory things about me in their status updates."

"What did Steve do? Did he explain that it was all a misunderstanding?"

"Are you kidding? He loved all the attention he was getting. There is such a double standard when it comes to guys and girls. His guy friends made him out to be a hero for coming between two close friends. The whole thing was—and still is—a nightmare."

"What about Charlotte—couldn't you get her alone and talk to her?"

Delilah smiled at River's choice of words "get her alone and talk." That's what got her in this predicament in the first place. "I really couldn't talk to her. She didn't want to see me."

"I would think that she wouldn't put a guy in front of your friendship," River said.

"Steve wasn't just a guy. He was—" she hesitated for a moment and looked at River. "He was her first." River stared back at her with a blank face, so she felt she had to say more. "You know. The first guy she ever slept with."

"I see," River said with a smile.

"Well, she confided in me about everything. If I had done what she thinks I did, she would have every right to hate me. Beyond the whole thing with Steve, Charlotte and I had been building up to a falling out for a while. We just hadn't been seeing things eye-to-eye for a long time."

"Let me guess—ever since Rachael came into the picture."

"Exactly. I think she was feeding Charlotte lies for a while, and the incident with Steve just confirmed everything for her."

"I'm sorry, Delilah. This whole situation is really messed up."

"You don't know the half of it. Things have gone from bad to worse. People have come out of the woodwork at school and have started spreading rumors about me. They literally shout profanities at me in the halls. Apparently it's considered socially acceptable to do that now."

"So the day I saw you running in the park—"

"I just didn't want to go to school and deal with the BS."

"Delilah, to have all of this on your plate and then to deal with your sister —"

"I was still friends with Charlotte when everything happened with my sister. That's why, no matter what happens, I will always be thankful that she helped me get through that." Delilah said realizing that she was crying.

"Is everything all right over here?" The waitress walked over, but when she saw Delilah crying, she rephrased her question. "Is everything all right with the food, I mean?"

"Yes, everything is fine," River responded. "Delilah, would you like anything else?"

"No, I'm good."

"Then just the check, please."

"I'm so embarrassed," she said, wiping away tears.

"Why?"

"I don't know. I hate being vulnerable. I mean, when we first met, I was beating up a thug with a brick," she said with a laugh.

"You *were* pretty badass that day. See, you are stronger than you think."

"Sometimes I think I'm the weakest person in the world," she said as they stood up to leave.

"Trust me, you're not." River put his forehead to hers. She looked up and kissed him on the lips.

"So, where would you like to go next?" River asked, holding her hand as they walked back to his car.

"Could we stay out all night?" Delilah asked.

"If that's what you want. Why? What's the matter?"

"I just don't feel like being around my mother tonight, that's all."

"Why? What's going on?" River stopped walking and turned to face her.

"I'm embarrassed to even say it out loud."

"Why?"

"She's planning a séance," Delilah said, giving River a grieved look.

"What?" River started to laugh.

"I know, I know. I can hardly say it out loud," she said as she covered her face with her hands.

"Don't be embarrassed. Some people actually believe in that sort of thing."

"I know, but I think it was dumb kid stuff," she said.

"Did you do that kind of thing when you were a kid?" he asked.

"Yes, and I'm not proud to admit it."

"What kind of things did you do?" River asked, sounding intrigued.

"You know, Ouija boards, table tilting…things like that," she said as they resumed walking to his car.

"Ouija boards?" River said, laughing. He hit the button to unlock the car and opened the passenger-side door. She couldn't remember the last time she saw a guy, especially one as young as River, open a car door for a woman.

"Thank you," she said, stepping inside and taking a deep breath. His car had that new-car smell that she loved. She snuck in another long, deep breath as he walked to the driver's side. Instead of starting the car when he got in, he sat and looked at her.

"What?" she said.

"Why is this bothering you so much?" he asked. "If you don't believe in it, what difference does it make?"

"What would you say if I told you that a part of me does believe in it?" she said, shifting her body to face River. "I believe in spirits and ghosts, and I've had some scary experiences in high school. I just don't think people should be messing with that stuff. Especially in my house, where I think …" she trailed off.

"Yes?"

"Well, it's just that a part of me does believe that my sister's spirit still resides in my house, and I don't like the idea of my mom messing with it. When I was a freshman in high school, Rachael introduced us to table tilting. She read a book or something about it, and she made us try it."

"Did something happen?" River asked.

"There was this one time when we met in Rachael's basement. It was a Saturday night and we were bored, so Rachael had the bright idea of communicating with the dead. It was like a scene out of a low-budget horror movie. It was a rainy night, and the five of us were all huddled around a small card table. We turned the lights off and Rachael lit some candles. Even though I was completely scared, I was even more afraid to stand up to Rachael and tell her that I didn't want to do it. I knew that Charlotte felt the same way, but she would never say anything."

"What happened?"

"We just went around the table calling out letters from the alphabet, waiting for the table to tilt and give us some type of message. We ended up spelling G-E-T-O-U-T-N-O-W."

"What?" River asked, sounding confused.

"Get out now! The whole thing was just completely freaky, and I never want to be put in a situation like that again."

"Thinking about it now, knowing what you know about Rachael, don't you think that maybe she set everything up?"

"I don't know. She seemed really scared herself, and she's not that good of an actress."

"Haven't you ever tried scaring someone and found that you only ended up scaring yourself?" he asked.

"I guess. Why? You don't think something like that would scare you?"

"No, that wouldn't scare me at all. I don't believe in that stuff."

"Are you saying that you don't believe in spirits or ghosts?"

"No, what I'm saying is I don't think you need a dark room, candles, or a toy like a Ouija board to conjure them."

"Why? What do you believe?"

"I believe that spirits are all around us, every day, everywhere we go."

"A part of me really wants to believe that, and another part of me is afraid that it's true."

"Why would you be afraid?" River asked.

"Well, it just sort of freaks me out to think that my dead grandfather could be an angel who's watching over me all the time, even when I'm taking a shower," she said with a laugh.

"Why do you think your angel has to be someone you knew?" River asked seriously.

"What?"

"I just think it's odd that whenever anyone talks about having a guardian angel, their angel is always someone they knew in this life."

"Why? What do you think?"

"Well, it's just that I always believed that a guardian angel could be someone that we've never met before. And it's not necessarily someone who is with you 24-7, watching your every move. I think it can be a stranger—someone you'd least expect, like that stranger who comes up to you on the street and stops to ask you for the time."

"What kind of guardian angel stops to ask for the time?" she asked.

"One who just saved your life," River said seriously.

"How could asking someone the time save that person's life?"

"It's not the asking that saves the person's life, but the act of stopping that person."

"Stopping them from what?"

"From crossing the intersection in front of a car that just ran the red light."

"So you're saying the guy who stops to give the time would never know what would have happened?"

"Not a clue. There would be no reason for him to know."

"Huh."

"What?" River asked.

"I never thought of it like that. Well, how about the poor guy who wasn't stopped and asked the time? He ends up looking like a pancake in the middle of the street."

"That person's time was probably done here on Earth."

"I guess. I do believe that everyone is put here for some purpose, no matter how short their time is here." Delilah could feel a lump well up in her throat as an image of Darcy came into her mind.

"I'm sorry. I didn't mean to get too deep," River said.

"No, I really like hearing your thoughts. They're comforting, somehow. I didn't know you were so philosophical."

"I took a philosophy course in college once. It was great. You could BS your way through the entire course. I ended up getting an A."

"I can see why. You're very convincing. Who used to talk to you about things like this? Was it your mom?"

"No, my mother didn't believe in anything at all. She was an atheist."

"From the way you talk, it seems like your mother may have influenced some of your beliefs."

"I guess it would be fair to say that she was the one who was responsible for my beliefs." River looked at Delilah intently and raised his brow. He lifted her chin with his hand and kissed her lips. Delilah leaned in and gave him a hug. She could feel him trembling.

Chapter 8

Delilah spent the whole week with River. She met up with him every day after school. The thought of seeing him helped her get through each day. It comforted her to know that she could vent to him about all the crap that she had been going through at school—and there had been a lot of crap. She cut school again yesterday; not wanting to deal with anyone. She especially didn't want to bump into Nora again and get another earful about the séance that was planned for tonight. Although, talking with River did help her realize that the séance wasn't that big of a deal, and that it might even give her mother some closure.

She wished River could be with her tonight, but he had an event to attend with his uncle. Instead, he had promised to spend the day with her in the city. She was meeting him at his uncle's place, and she hoped that he would introduce her to someone, anyone, in his family. There was so much more that she wanted to know about him, but he was so vague whenever he spoke—especially about his family. Delilah hoped to shed some light on that subject today, although she didn't want to appear too nosy. After all, she still hadn't told him what happened to her sister, and he hadn't asked any questions. She really liked that about him—he was so patient and cool. He let her know that he was there for her if she wanted to talk, but she never felt pressured into telling him anything that she wasn't comfortable talking about. She tried to take his lead and act the same way, but it was hard for her. She surmised that she just wasn't as cool as he was.

It was a beautiful day, and Delilah enjoyed the short walk from the train to the building. River was waiting for her when she arrived. He was wearing a pair of jeans and a gray button-down shirt. His hair was a bit tousled, but he looked good.

Delilah wasn't very anxious to see his uncle's place since he'd only been living there for the past few months. She would rather visit his brother's house in Florida or the house he shared with his mother—those were the places where he had set down roots. But maybe his aunt or cousin would come home while she was visiting and she would have the chance to meet them.

The doorman greeted them warmly as they entered the building. "Good afternoon, Mr. Carter."

"Good afternoon, Jack."

"Why did he call you Mr. Carter?" Delilah asked River as they stepped into the elevator.

"Because he knows that Robert Carter is my uncle, so I guess he just assumes we have the same last name. It must not have occurred to him that I could be the child of my uncle's sister and have a different last name."

His uncle's apartment was on the fourteenth floor. Delilah was really impressed with what she saw. It was very big and decorated with a lot of ornate, expensive-looking objects. She didn't have much experience with the finer things in life, but reality TV had shown her how the other half lived. She was suddenly a little embarrassed by her own home and how shabby it must have looked to River after staying in such a nice place. For a moment she closed her eyes and tried to imagine what it would be like to be married to River and living in this place. She would love to spend nights lying by the fire with him, drinking wine or scotch, whatever it was that rich people drank.

She tried not to look too obvious as she walked around checking the place out. She noticed some pictures on the mantle; her eyes settled on a picture that must have been of his uncle and aunt on the beach. It looked like they were on vacation: there were palm trees in the background and his aunt had a lei around her neck. Hawaii — the place her parents always wanted to go but had never been able to afford. She suddenly felt very sorry for her parents and how unfair their lives had been. Her poor mother would probably settle for a trip to Coney Island if it meant that she could be with her dad.

River gave her a quick tour of the apartment, and, as she expected, it didn't give her any more insight into his life. She wanted to see his home, the home where he was raised. There were no pictures of him from Little League games or an old bedroom of his to visit. Even though she knew that she didn't have the nicest house on the block, at least there were memories from her childhood — although not all the memories were good ones.

Delilah got the impression that River wasn't very comfortable hanging out in his uncle's apartment, because they didn't stay very long. He said he wanted to get out and enjoy the day. They ended up doing some window-shopping on Madison Avenue. River got a kick out of her enthusiasm for shopping. He smiled as she gawked and drooled over things she couldn't afford. After a few hours, River said that he had to go back to the apartment and get ready for the event that evening with his uncle and his uncle's associates. Delilah was disappointed, and secretly thought about how she would love to join him. Instead, she would have to find something else to do.

When Delilah got back home, she could hear her mother on the phone speaking to Nora's mother, Claire. Her insides were churning. She walked down the hall and found her mother flipping through a book, bending her neck to hold the phone with her shoulder, totally disregarding her chiropractor's advice.

"According to my book, it says that we should all wear something lavender-scented. The spirits are attracted to that."

"What are you doing?" Delilah asked, sounding miffed.

Susan looked up, confused. "What?"

"You know what I mean," Delilah said.

"Claire, I'm going to have to call you back later," Susan said before switching off the cordless phone. "Now, would you please tell me what your problem is?"

"This is my problem!" Delilah said, taking the book out of her hands.

"Since when do you have a problem with my books about the spirit world? I've been reading them ever since—"

"I know you've been reading them ever since Darcy died, but that was almost three years ago, Mom! You have to stop all of this!"

"You just don't understand — and I pray to God that you never do have to understand!"

"How can you say that I don't understand? You have no idea what I've been going through these past few years, Mom!" Delilah said, bursting into tears. "I'm the one who is responsible for her accident!"

"Please, please don't say that! It was no one's fault. It just happened."

"That's not what I overheard you telling Daddy the night Darcy died."

"Oh dear God, Delilah, honey, I had no idea that you heard Daddy and me talking that night."

"That's right, Mom, I heard! I heard the whole thing, and I've been living with this guilt for years!

"D, sweetheart, you have to understand that this was no one's fault, it just happened. It was an accident, and I know ... I know ..." Susan began crying and her nose was running like a faucet. "I know that your sister knows it was a simple accident, too. In fact, she jokingly blamed herself."

"What do you mean, she knows it was an accident and she blames herself? Darcy is *dead*! She can't talk to you anymore, Mom! I know that you want to believe that, but it's simply not true!"

"It *is* true!" Susan said adamantly. "I do talk to her, and tonight I am going to prove it!"

"To whom, Mom? Nora and her simple-minded mother? You could probably get those two to believe in the tooth fairy and unicorns!"

"Please, please join us tonight and you'll see—I don't know if it will work, I don't know if she'll be willing to speak to everyone, but if you'll just—"

"It's not her, Mom! I'm sorry, but it's true. I don't know whose voice you're hearing, but your mind can play a lot of tricks on you. You're just hearing what you want to hear."

"I don't just hear her, I see her," her mother whispered. "I see her, and she's so beautiful. She looks almost exactly the same, except for her eyes. There's something different about her eyes." Susan continued talking as if she's trying to convince herself. "Her eyes ..."

"I can't take this any longer!" Delilah interrupted. "Please stop!" She heard her mother yelling out to her as she ran into her room and closed the door.

She threw herself on the bed and sobbed into her pillow. *I just can't do this anymore. I can't deal with her when she's like this. I have to see my dad. I need to talk to him and see what he thinks about this. We are going to have to commit my mother.*

Delilah rang her dad's doorbell only once before he answered. He was wearing a white T-shirt and his uniform pants. A couple of months ago, he took a weekend job doing security work. He claimed he needed the extra cash, but Delilah thought he got a job to keep busy on Saturday nights. He and her mom used to go to the movies together on Saturday nights. Delilah couldn't believe it, but he looked like he had aged at least five years in the last week.

"What's up, kiddo?" he said, throwing his arms around her.

"Hi, Daddy," she said as she hugged him back. She had forgotten how much she liked to hug him. They didn't hug a lot when he was living at home. In fact, she noticed that they stopped hugging around the time she became a teenager. Now that she thought of it, maybe she was the one that stopped hugging him.

"I know you don't have a lot of time before heading out to work, but I don't think that this can wait."

"Are you kidding? I always have time for you. What's going on? You sounded pretty frantic on the phone."

"It's Mom. Do you know what she has planned for tonight?"

"Oh, you mean the séance?"

"You know?" Delilah said, surprised.

"Yes, she told me a few weeks ago that she planned on having it."

"You knew about this and you didn't try to do anything to stop it?" Delilah said disconcertingly.

"What's the harm in it?"

"Gee, I don't know, Dad, don't you feel a bit like an enabler? We should be working together to discourage her from these types of things."

"I think that if this makes your mother happy, then we should support her."

"What? This whole thing is crazy."

"Delilah, listen to me. Sometimes I think that neither of us gives your mother enough credit. We both know that she had a problem with alcohol before all of this happened with your sister." Delilah couldn't believe that her father was saying these things out loud. They never openly discussed her mother's drinking problem. It wasn't until she started AA, shortly after Darcy's death, that they even acknowledged she had a problem. It's sad that it took a death in the family for her mother to sober up. "I think it's wonderful that your mother has been able to stay sober this long. That couldn't have been easy on her."

"I know that. But the way she's acting now— it's crazy!"

"D, I want you to stop this right now! Your mother is fine. I was with her just two nights ago."

"You were?" She had no idea that her parents had seen each other at all.

"Yes, and she's doing great. She's completely sober and she firmly believes that she's developed some sort of sixth sense. She claims that she even gets strange feelings when she's not in our house."

"You mean she's convinced herself that she's some type of medium now?"

"My point is that if all she wants is for us to show her a little support with this whole thing, I think that's the least we could do."

"I don't understand. I thought all this stuff drove you nuts."

"Your mother and I just needed some time apart. There are a lot of things that we need to work out. We're still trying. I still love your mother very much, and I want to be there for her if she needs me."

Suddenly Delilah felt guilty. *Maybe I should have been more understanding instead of making Mom feel like she's crazy.* Delilah had to admit that there was a small part of her that was afraid her mother might be right. It had always been easier for her to believe that her mother was just delusional with grief than to believe that her deceased sister was still with them.

"I'm sorry, Dad," she said as she fell back on the couch. She put her head in her hands and sighed. "I just worry about her sometimes, you know?"

"I know, sweetie. I worry about her, too. We're a family, and families are supposed to worry about each other. No matter how big you get, I will always worry about you."

"I know, Daddy, and I love you for that."

"I love you, too."

"I better let you finish getting ready for work."

"Okay. I'll stop by this week to check in on you."

"Thanks, Dad," she said as she got up and headed for the door. "By the way, Dad, do you believe in all this stuff?"

"To be honest, I don't know. I do believe in your mother, and if she feels this strongly about everything, then maybe there is some truth to it," her father said. Delilah smiled at him and gave him one last hug before walking away. As Delilah walked back to her house, River called her cell.

"Hey, what's up?"

"Hi, I'm just checking in," he said.

"Are you calling from the restaurant?"

"No. I was just about to leave. Delilah, are you all right? You sound upset."

"I'm fine. I just came from seeing my dad. We spoke about what my mom has planned for tonight."

"What did he have to say?"

"Actually, he also told me that she needs to do this—for closure."

"I'm sure she'll get the closure that she needs after tonight," River said.

"I hope you're right."

"Trust me," River said. "I'm glad you and your dad seem to be in a good place."

"Yes, we are. I have to say I was really surprised by how understanding he was."

"That's how my dad was. I always felt like I could tell him anything and he would never judge me."

"You sound like you really miss your dad," Delilah said. *For someone who only knew him for such a short time.*

"Yes, I do. Anyway, Delilah, I'd better get going. I really wish that I could be with you tonight."

"I know you do. I wish that I could be with you too."

"Are you sure you're going to be okay tonight?"

"Yes, I'll be fine. I'll find something else to do while my mother is entertaining."

"Okay. I'll call you tomorrow."

"Okay."

"Oh, and Delilah … I love you." He didn't give her a chance to respond. He just hung up.

Delilah sat in her room, thinking about River and all the questions she still had. He just told her that he loved her, and she wanted to believe it was true. She also wanted to believe the stories he had been telling her about his family, but for some reason, she couldn't shake the feeling that he was hiding something. She needed to find out more. She decided to do a little sleuthing on the Internet, and locked herself in her room so she wouldn't be disturbed.

Delilah was only on the computer a couple of minutes when she heard the doorbell ring. *You have got to be kidding me. I guess Nora and her mother decided to grace us with their presence a little early tonight.* She stepped away from her computer, walked over to her window, and pulled back the curtain. She saw Nora and her mother, Claire, waiting on the front porch. They're wearing very similar jackets and standing so close together that they look like conjoined twins. They had such an odd relationship. As she stood there staring, she could hear her mother open the front door. As Claire greeted Susan with a hug, Nora spied Delilah through the window. It was like she knew that Delilah had been watching her the whole time, but didn't want to give her the satisfaction of looking back. Feeling almost frightened, Delilah quickly drew the curtains closed. *She is so weird. No wonder tonight is completely up her alley.*

Delilah sat back down in front of her computer, feeling guilty as she began to type River's father's name in the search box. She couldn't believe what she was doing. "What am I going to do once I find him? Pay him a visit and tell him that I've been dating the son he abandoned?" Before she even finished typing, she decided that she couldn't do it. She got up from the computer and lied down on her bed, staring at the ceiling for a few minutes. She felt a little tired, so she closed her eyes.

Suddenly, she jumped up. She was sweating, her throat was dry, and she felt like she was suffocating. It was dark, and her heart was racing. Her pulse was banging in her ears. It took a few seconds, which felt like hours, for her to realize that she was still in her own room. She looked at the clock and it was 3:04 in the morning. *I must have fallen asleep. I have to get out of this room.*

She felt like she was going to crawl out of her own skin. Leaning over, she turned on the lamp that was on her nightstand and grabbed a hair band. She walked over to the mirror hanging on the wall. She pulled her wet hair off her face and twisted it into a bun. Studying her reflection for a moment, she lifted her hand, and ran her fingers down the front of her neck.

"You have got to calm down," she said to herself. As she turned toward her nightstand to grab a bottle of water, an image of a young girl appeared in the mirror. She was wearing a long white dress and she was smiling. Delilah turned around and caught a quick glimpse of the image in the mirror before it vanished. She dropped the bottle and vigorously rubbed her eyes. *My mind is playing tricks on me.* She walked toward her bedroom door and opened it. She heard a loud scream; it took her a moment to realize that the sound was coming from her own throat.

Chapter 9

Her mother was standing right outside her door. She was wearing a long white nightgown similar to the image Delilah saw in her mirror. She wasn't expecting her mother to be standing right there in front of her at that time in the morning.

"Delilah, honey, I'm sorry for scaring you," her mother said.

"Oh my God! You almost gave me a heart attack! What are you doing? You do realize that it's after three in the morning, don't you?"

"Yes. I'm sorry. I was just about to come in and check on you, but you opened the door first."

"Are you in the habit of checking on me in the middle of the night?" Delilah asked.

"Actually, I am." Susan said with a weird smile. "Can we talk?"

"I guess so, but wouldn't you rather wait until the sun comes up?"

"No—this really can't wait," Susan, said.

"What's going on? You're starting to freak me out."

"I don't mean to freak you out, D. I just want to talk. Let's sit down on your bed."

"Sure. Why not? It's not unusual to have a heart-to-heart talk at three in the morning," Delilah muttered. "Well?" she said, trying to encourage her mother to spit it out already.

"I want to talk to you about the morning your sister—" Susan stopped for a minute and took a long breath. "The morning of your sister's accident."

"Oh God, Mom, please don't start this again. I can't keep talking about this. I'm never going to be able to move on with my life if you keep bringing up that morning."

"Well, maybe I can tell you something about it that will help you to move on."

"What? What can you tell me about the accident that I don't already know? Because here is what I do know: I didn't protect her like I should have. I was embarrassed and I used to put her out of my mind—the same way I put her out of my mind the night I left the basement door open. The door that Daddy warned me about closing time and time again. 'Close the door and don't forget to latch the safety lock.' I can hear his voice now. I swear,

Mom, I thought I closed that door behind me. I went over it again and again in my mind."

"You did."

"What?"

"You did close the door that night. I saw you do it before you went to bed."

"How do you know?"

"I was watching you. I was watching you very closely, because I was waiting for you to go to bed."

"What? Why?"

"Because I wanted to drink. I wanted to drink, but I didn't want to do it in front of you. I went downstairs right after you went to bed, and I opened my special cabinet where I had my bottles discreetly hidden behind some old records that used to belong to your grandfather. I knew that no one would ever move those things, so I used to hide all of my alcohol back there. I remember, D. I remember all too well."

"What happened next?" Delilah whispered.

"I drank. I just sat on that old beanbag chair that we used to have and I drank."

"So you just sat there and got drunk?"

"I didn't just get drunk. I was thinking. You know my drinking time was also my thinking time."

"What were you thinking about?"

"About you, your father, and your sister. You know, D, I was very young when I had you. I always dreamt of going to college and becoming a lawyer, but shortly after your father and I met, I got pregnant with you."

"Thanks a lot. So I guess I was an accident."

"You weren't an accident. You were a surprise."

"What's the difference?" Delilah asked.

"Well, they're both something that you don't expect, but an accident is something you wouldn't do again if you could. But a surprise, a surprise like you, is something that I would never change. After I had you, your father and I got married and my priorities changed. I went to work as a secretary, and I was content for a little while until I decided I wanted more. I was planning on going back to college to pursue that law degree that I always wanted, but just as I was about to make that happen, we found out that we were having surprise number two."

"Darcy," Delilah said.

"At first I wasn't sure how I felt about it, but then I would look at you and how beautiful you were. How beautiful you are. I've always been so proud of you. I thought to myself, it's going to be okay. And it was. Darcy was such a beautiful baby. She was so smart—you could always tell what she was thinking just by looking at her. She had a sparkle in her eyes that was like a light. And then, one day, the light just went out. I don't know why or how. It just happened, and suddenly she was faced with so many challenges. God, Delilah, there were just so many damn challenges. I used to hide a lot of what the doctors told us from you, because I didn't want you to worry. I even hid some things from your father because I knew that he couldn't handle it."

"Oh, and you were doing such a bang-up job of handling things on your own? Sneaking down to the basement and getting drunk?"

"You're right. I guess I deserve that. I used to depend on the bottle to help me get through things. I just had so much to deal with. Taking care of your sister was a full-time job, and I knew that I had to live with the fact that I would never go to college. Plus, the bills were piling up. I guess on that night things really came to a head and hit me hard. Your sister had had a hard day, and I was both mentally and physically exhausted. I was just so tired."

"What, Mom? What happened next?"

"I don't really remember exactly. That night I went back upstairs. I can remember stumbling a few times as I tried to reach the top. Somehow I made it into my bed and the next morning, I awoke to a blood-curdling yell. It was your father. I left the basement door open the night before. I was too drunk to even close it. When your father went to get

Darcy up the next morning, she must have gone looking for me. She tried going down the steps but she wasn't very coordinated. The doctors said she probably just lost her footing. You know the rest— the coroner's report said she broke her neck. Oh God, I killed her! I killed my baby girl!"

"What are you saying? That you did it on purpose? That you left that door open knowing that she would go looking for you downstairs?"

"No!"

"You knew that Daddy got Darcy out of bed every Saturday morning, and you knew that she would go looking for you in the basement where you usually were on a Saturday morning, doing laundry, or so we thought. You were probably just down there drinking."

"No. How could you even think that? I would never do something like that intentionally."

"I don't know what to think anymore, Mom. With both of us out of the picture, you could do whatever the hell you wanted!"

"It wasn't a murder, Delilah. It was an accident."

"An accident that you let me believe was my fault!" Delilah yelled.

"I swear, Delilah, I didn't even know that you knew about that. I had no idea that you overheard Daddy and me talking."

"What kind of person does that? How could you let my father believe…?" Delilah could barely get the words out.

"I'm so sorry, baby. You just don't understand."

"No, I think you're the one who doesn't understand. Do you know how guilty I felt after hearing you say that? I actually believed that maybe I subconsciously left the door open on purpose because I was embarrassed of her."

"I know you wouldn't have done that."

"I don't know, Mom, maybe we're more alike than you think. I became pretty selfish there, too, for a while. You know how I had my whole social world going on. I thought that was the only thing that mattered. I couldn't stand the thought of my sister being different and people making fun of me or her because of it."

"Don't talk like that! You were a great sister — the best." Susan was sobbing. "You used to protect her."

"Well, I didn't do a very good job of it — I mean, look what happened! I guess it was you I should have been protecting her from the whole time."

"How can you say that?"

"How can I say that?" Delilah repeated. "You just admitted that you were drunk. Maybe you didn't leave the door open intentionally, but if you had been sober, you would have remembered to close it and protect your child."

"I know, Delilah, and I think about that every day of my life. That's why I haven't had a drink since the accident."

"How do we know that's even true? You were always able to hide your drinking so well. How do I know that you're not still drinking?"

"I'm not. I swear to you!"

"How could you blame me for Darcy's accident?"

"I had to do that. If I told your father the truth, he would never have forgiven me. It's like you said—I was a drunk. But you—you, D—he's always adored you. I knew that he would never blame you for the accident, and he didn't."

"How ... do ... you ... know? You have no idea what he's thinking. He probably blames me every time he looks at me."

"No, Delilah, sweetheart, he doesn't. It was just an accident. It could have happened to anyone."

"Does thinking that help you get through the night?" Delilah said callously.

"No, because in my case alcohol played a part in my actions. In your case, you just weren't paying attention."

"God, do you hear yourself?

"I'm so sorry for what I told your father. He's the only one I told that to, and I swear I never wanted you to find out about it. Had I known that you thought you were really responsible for it, I would have said something a long time ago."

"Yeah, Mom, I wish you would have said something a long time ago. I've gone a really long time thinking that I'm some kind of monster—not just because I left a door open, because honestly, that could happen to anyone, but because I thought deep down inside of myself, maybe I did it on purpose."

"Don't say that. You know it's not true!"

"Why not? You told me once that I would have to be the one to care for her when she got older. I could barely care for her as a child, let alone as an adult."

"Stop. Just stop saying these things. I know you're doing it to upset me, and I'm sorry for all of this. I just don't know what else to say."

"You're right, Mom, I am saying a lot of this to make you feel guilty and to make you think some of the crazy thoughts that have been going through my head the past few years, even if I know now they're not true. I honestly don't know if you could handle all the pain *I've* been feeling for the past few years, at least not while you're sober."

"Delilah, I'm sorry. I will make everything up to you."

"Make it up to me! How? Do you know that after Charlotte stopped talking to me along with, well, basically the whole school, I tried to kill myself?"

"Oh God, Delilah, no!"

"That's right. Charlotte was the only person I used to confide in. Once she thought I betrayed her, she shut me out and so did everyone else. I felt truly alone."

"Delilah, you always had me and your father."

"You were both in such a fragile state. I didn't want to come to you with my problems. After all, I thought my problems were so trivial compared to yours. I mean, you lost a daughter, and it was because of me. How could I expect you to both feel sorry for me? Actually, I thought you were some type of angel to not resent me for what happened. In fact, thinking of you and Daddy and Darcy and the happy times we spent together, that's what made me stick my fingers down my throat and regurgitate the entire bottle of pills."

"If something would have happened to you, I would have died."

"I know."

"D, I love you so much. I am so sorry for all of this. I want to make things right again. How can I make it up to you?"

"Well, you can start by telling Daddy the truth," Delilah said.

"I will. I promise you I will. I'll do it today."

"Fine. But just tell me one thing. Why? Why now? Why is it that you've decided to confess to all this crap at three o'clock on a Sunday morning?"

Susan arched her brow and momentarily hesitated to speak.

"Oh, don't tell me. The séance. Did Darcy come through and tell you to tell me the truth? News flash, Mom, it wasn't Darcy who was tipping your table, it was Nora or Claire or both of those fruitcakes working in cahoots."

"No, you were right. Nothing happened. I guess I was hoping for something. Something she could say to give me closure. And when that didn't happen, I realized I had to be responsible for my own closure. So here I am."

"I don't believe it. There's something you're not telling me. There's a reason that you decided to tell me this now and a reason you are going to talk to Daddy today."

"I'm sorry if you don't believe me, D, but there is something I want you to know. I may have lied to your father about what happened, but that was only because I wanted to keep this family together."

"If you say you did it for me ..."

"I just want you to know that I love you very much and I never lied to you. You and your sister were my best gifts, my two surprises. Even now, I would never change having both of you in my life."

Delilah looked at her for a moment with a blank stare. "Don't talk to Daddy today," she said coldly. "He said that he'd be here on Wednesday for dinner. I want to tell him then, when we're together."

"Whatever you want, baby." Susan closed the door gently. Delilah could hear her crying as she walked down the hallway.

Delilah felt like her head was about to explode. She wanted to talk to River, but it wasn't even four o'clock yet. *Damn it!* There was no way she'd be able to go back to sleep. She looked over at her laptop; she had left it on sleep mode. She walked over to her desk and opened it. The light from the computer screen was so bright it hurt her eyes. Taking a long, deep breath, she typed Robert Spencer, Attorney at Law in the search box. It only took a moment for an address to pop up onto the screen. She closed her eyes, and pondered her next move.

First thing Monday morning Delilah was on a train heading for the city. She spent the previous day locked in her room listening to The Best of Nickelback that she had downloaded to her iPod. She was able to avoid her mother for most of the day, and she only spoke to River briefly on the phone. She needed that time alone—time to plan what she was now about to do.

At eight o'clock she got off the train. She spent the ride imagining how she would burst into River's father's law office, demanding answers. As she approached the law office wearing her black pantsuit, the one she's only worn once before to her Aunt Virginia's funeral, she thought to herself how crazy this whole thing was. She was proud of herself for making it this far. She felt stronger somehow, more in control of her own life and actions.

When she stepped off the elevator, she saw a robust-looking young man sitting behind a desk. "Hello? May I help you?" he asked.

"Yes, I would like to see Robert Spencer," she said rather confidently. She honestly didn't know how she was mustering the nerve to do this. If this had been just one day ago, she probably wouldn't be standing here right now. But after everything that happened with her mother, she felt like she had nothing left to lose. She had no one left to depend on; if she was going to become stronger, she had better learn to depend on herself. Tomorrow was Tuesday; and the plan was to go back to school and use some of her newfound fortitude to stand up to Rachael and the Imitators. It was time to get her life back in some kind of order.

"Do you have an appointment with Mr. Spencer?" the receptionist asked.

"No, I'm afraid that I don't, but I was hoping to meet with him for a few minutes. It's about a personal matter."

"Oh, I see. Well, I'll just need to check with Mr. Spencer's secretary." As the receptionist reached for the phone, Delilah heard a ding; it was the sound of the elevator doors opening. "Well, speak of the devil. That's Mr. Spencer getting off the elevator now."

Delilah felt her knees beginning to buckle. She never imagined him stepping off of an elevator and approaching her; she envisioned having the upper hand and surprising *him* as she burst through his office doors. As he stepped off the elevator, she could see that he was a man of distinction. He was tall with salt-and-pepper hair and an attractive, careworn face. He was holding hands with a woman who seemed to be about the same age as him. She was also tall and very attractive, with long blonde hair that looked like it belonged on someone half her age.

"Mr. Spencer is with his wife right now. Would you like me to ask his secretary to schedule a private meeting for you at another time?"

"No, that's quite all right. I would really like to meet with him now, if he will see me." At that moment Delilah didn't care about Mr. Spencer or his wife—she just wanted answers.

"Ahem," the receptionist cleared his throat as Mr. Spencer approached the front desk. "Good morning, Mr. Spencer, Mrs. Spencer."

"Simon." Robert's voice was steady and cool.

"Mr. Spencer, this young lady is waiting to meet with you."

"Does she have an appointment?" he asked, not even looking at Delilah.

"No, but she says it's personal." Mrs. Spencer's eyes darted toward her. She gave Delilah a warm smile. Delilah smiled back.

"That's fine, Simon, thank you." Robert Spencer turned to Delilah. "Please follow me," he said calmly.

Delilah could feel her heart in her throat, but she followed them calmly through the double doors and down a long hallway.

"I'll wait for you in the lounge," Mrs. Spencer said to her husband. "We can go over those documents for my grandmother's estate later."

"Let me just see how long this matter will take," Robert said while holding the door open for Delilah.

"Well the matter that I would like to discuss is actually about you and your family," Delilah said.

"In that case, would it be all right if my wife joins us?"

"Yes, that would be all right," Delilah said, not convinced that was the best idea. Robert held his office door open.

His office was very nice—warm and inviting. Delilah could tell right away that his wife must have helped decorate; it definitely had a woman's touch. His wife took a seat on a small floral sofa that was placed at the far end of the room.

"Please, have a seat." Robert pulled out a chair and waited for Delilah to sit.

"Thank you," she said, her voice trembling. "I'm sorry to come by without an appointment." Delilah looked over at Mrs. Spencer. She hadn't expected her to be here when she planned her speech to Mr. Spencer. She had intended to start off by demanding, "Why did you abandon your son?" She hadn't wanted to tell River, but she suspected that his mother had a hand in keeping him and his father apart.

"So I seem to be at a disadvantage. You know my name, but I don't know yours," Robert Spencer said as he lifted his pant leg and informally took a seat on the edge of his desk.

"Yes, I'm sorry. I'm Delilah."

"Do you have a last name, Delilah?"

"Yes. Simms."

"Well, what kind of personal matter would you like to discuss with me, Ms. Simms?" Delilah got the distinct impression that he wasn't taking her very seriously, probably because she looked young.

"Um …," she hesitated and looked at Mrs. Spencer, who was sitting with her legs crossed tightly as she stared back intensely at Delilah.

"Ms. Simms, please just say what you came to say."

"Well—" just as she was about to talk, the telephone rang.

"Excuse me one moment," Mr. Spencer said as he leaned across his desk and picked up the phone. "Okay, that's fine. I will tell my wife. Thank you for calling." He hung up and said to his wife, "Darling, that was Darcy's school. The afterschool program was canceled, so you'll have to pick her up at the main building, regular time." He turned back to Delilah. "I'm sorry about that, Ms. Simms. Now you were just about to tell us what you came to discuss."

"Darcy? Who's Darcy?" Delilah asked.

"Darcy is our daughter," Mrs. Spencer said. "Why do you ask, dear?"

"I'm sorry. I must appear dreadfully nosy." Delilah tried to match their sophisticated tone. "It's just that I had a little sister named Darcy."

"You *had* a sister named Darcy," Mr. Spencer said sounding confused.

"Yes, she … uh, passed away a few years ago."

"Oh, my dear, I'm very sorry for your loss," Mrs. Spencer said sympathetically.

"So getting back to the matter at hand," Mr. Spencer said, looking at Delilah.

"I'm sorry," Delilah said, squeezing her hands tightly in her lap and taking a deep breath. "I came to talk about River." After she said his name, she held her breath and looked at their faces, waiting for a response.

"River? What about River?" *Well at least he knows who he is, and he hasn't thrown Mrs. Spencer out of the room yet.*

"River—he's your son, isn't he? I mean, I was just wondering—or, that is to say, we were just wondering—"

"Who is 'we'?" he asked, disconcerted.

"Well, River and me. He told me all about you and your relationship with him."

"What did he tell you?" Mr. Spencer asked. He saw Delilah look hesitantly over at his wife and said, "It's all right. Tell me what you came to say."

Delilah could feel the tension in the room. She started to think that this was a terrible idea. She wanted to run out of the room, but she pressed on. "I'm not sure what River's mother told you about him, but River would very much like to see you."

"River wants to see me. Is that what you're telling me?"

"Yes, and—"

"When was the last time you spoke to him?"

"I speak to him all the time. You see I'm sort of his … his girlfriend."

"His *girlfriend*?"

"Yes, and—"

"Ms. Simms, I don't know what this is about or what kind of game you're playing, but I would appreciate it if you would leave my office right now."

"What are you talking about? I'm not playing any game, I just thought—"

"Good-bye, Ms. Simms." Mr. Spencer stood up and opened the door.

"Wait … please … I just thought that if you would be willing to see him again, maybe—"

"Ms. Simms, my son, River, is *dead*!"

"Oh my God, she must have been even crazier than I thought. Is that what she told you? River's mother, I mean? That he's dead?"

"Ms. Simms, please leave my office!"

"Don't you see what she did? She just told you that because she didn't want you in his life! Or maybe it's just what—Mr. Spencer, do you think I could speak to you alone?"

"I can leave so the two of you can talk," Mrs. Spencer said.

"You are not the one who is leaving," Mr. Spencer said to his wife. "Now, Ms. Simms, if you would kindly leave my office before I have you escorted out."

"I'm sorry, Mr. Spencer, but I just can't help but think that maybe the story about River dying was concocted to give your wife some closure. You know, since you had an affair with River's mother."

"That was a very long time ago and my wife is aware of my indiscretion," he said, sounding irritated.

"I just don't understand this whole thing," Delilah said, glancing over at some photos that were displayed on a bookshelf. "Is that a picture of you and River?" she said.

"Yes, that was them on a fishing trip when he was just four years old," Mrs. Spencer said. "Are you all right, dear?" Mrs. Spencer seemed sympathetic.

"Mr. Spencer, I just have to ask—" She was interrupted by the sound of an intercom.

"Mr. Spencer, I have a Mr. Bergman for you on line one," a nasal sounding voice said.

"Thank you, Marcia. Please tell him to hold. Ms. Simms, I'm a very busy man and I don't have time for this, so if you would be so kind as to see yourself out of the building, or I can have Simon see you out—"

"Don't worry, Mr. Spencer, I can see myself out," Delilah said abruptly.

"I'll see you to the hall," he said.

"By the way," Delilah turned to face him. "You can drop the act. Your wife isn't here anymore. I'm not crazy. I can prove to you that River is alive if you're really interested, but obviously it's easier for you to pretend that he's dead. I guess that gives you and your family some type of closure, an acceptable way out of your illegitimate son's life."

"Ms. Simms—"

"You know, I was only here trying to do a nice thing for someone I really care about, and I'm really sorry if I've taken up too much of your time." Delilah turned and walked away in a huff.

Walking back into his office, Robert Spencer ignored his wife and the red flashing light on the phone. He wiped his forehead and sat down behind his desk. He pulled out his wallet, flipped through some recent photos, and stopped at a picture of himself and River. It was taken last year.

Chapter 10

By the time Delilah got home she felt like she was going to collapse from a combination of stress and lack of sleep. She hesitated for a moment before turning the key to her front door. Her mother was probably home, and Delilah didn't know how she would react when she saw her. Despite everything, she was still the only person that Delilah wanted to talk to — not just because she was literally the only person she *could* talk to right now, but because she genuinely wanted to speak with her and tell her about meeting with River's father.

When Delilah walked in the front door, she saw her mother's feet hanging off the edge of the sofa. For a moment she felt scared. She ran inside and saw her mother sprawled out on the sofa with her arms over her head.

"Mom! Mom!" Delilah said shaking her mother's arm.

"D … Delilah, honey, is that you?" Susan said groggily.

"Yes, Mom, it's me. You scared me."

"You've seen me napping on the couch before," she said sitting up and smoothing her hair with her hands.

"I know, it's just that—"

"It's just that you thought I was drunk or took a bottle of pills. I'm sorry, D, but I'm not going to let you get rid of me that easily."

"Stop that." *Leave it to my mother to try to make me feel guilty after what she's done.*

"I can't say that I'd blame you if you did have some bad thoughts about me."

"Mom, I haven't had any bad thoughts about you. I have other things going on in my life right now," Delilah said as she nudged Susan's legs so she would make room for her on the couch.

"What? What is it? Did something else happen with those girls?" Susan took the blanket off her lap and wrapped it around Delilah's shoulders. Delilah felt warm and safe and tried to put everything from this morning out of her mind.

"No, it's not them," Delilah said as she pushed her body up against the back of the couch and folded her legs beneath her.

"Where did you go?" Susan asked calmly. There was a part of Delilah that wanted to tell her that it was none of her business, but when she looked into her mother's swollen, weepy eyes, she could tell that Susan must have been crying all day.

"I went to see River's father," Delilah blurted out.

"River's father?" Susan repeated, surprised.

"Yes, he's a lawyer in Manhattan. His office isn't too far from where River has been working with his uncle."

"I thought you told me that his father had abandoned him as a child," she said anxiously.

"He did. I just thought that I could —"

"You just thought that you could track down his father and reunite them after all these years?"

"Yes, that's what I wanted, but it didn't work out that way."

"I'm sure it didn't," her mother said.

"Why do you say it like that? There was a chance that he might have wanted to see him again."

"I know, honey, but ..."

"But what?"

"Well, it's just that if his dad is a lawyer and only works a few blocks from where River is working, I'm sure he would have reached out to River himself if he wanted to."

"I know. His father was being a real jerk. I guess he's content with his life the way it is. He has a wife that he seems really into and a daughter. The daughter's name is Darcy."

"D ... D ... Darcy?" Susan stuttered.

"I know. It's a coincidence, right?"

"Yes. Yes, it is," her mother stammered. "How odd that you and River both have a sister with the same name."

"You're right. I didn't even think of it like that. Darcy would be his half-sister. I wonder if he even knows that she exists."

"Maybe he does."

"I'm not so sure. I mean how would he? It's been years since he's seen his dad."

"Well, maybe his mother told him that he has a sister," Susan said.

"That lunatic! She would never tell him that. I think that she's the one who told River's father that River died."

"What?" Susan said, sitting up straighter.

"Yeah. He actually told me that River was dead. Either he was just trying to get rid of me or he's convinced himself that it's true. Either way it was obvious to me that this guy never really cared too much for his son if he was willing to believe something like that so easily—especially from a woman who River himself said was completely erratic. He was probably just looking for an easy way out of his son's life, which River's mother gave him on a silver platter. I bet River's uncle helped to tie up any loose ends. He's also a lawyer, and River's mother was his sister. He could have helped to make it look like River had an accident and died. And considering his dad really didn't care all that much, he probably took their word for it. I mean who knows what kind of story they could have concocted? I even thought of a scenario where River's father was part of it. Maybe he was in cahoots with River's mother. He plays along that River is dead, and she stays out of his life. His wife is happy, River's mother is happy, and no one has to see each other again. It's a win-win situation."

"Wow, I see that you have given this a lot of thought. You must really care about River to get so involved. I mean, it was a really brave thing, doing what you did—going downtown and confronting his father."

"Thank you. I was proud of myself. I didn't know that I had it in me. To be honest, I've been doing a lot of things lately that I didn't know I had in me."

"Maybe you're a lot stronger than you thought," Susan said. Delilah could feel her eyes filling with tears. She knew that she was thinking about what Delilah told her earlier about trying to take her own life. "D, do you ever think that certain people come into our lives when we need them the most?"

"Yes, I guess so. I mean, it happens all the time. People come in and out of our lives."

"Sometimes people can save our lives without us even knowing it," Susan said.

"You're starting to sound like River."

"Why? What did River tell you?"

"He's very philosophical. He almost seems wiser than his years," Delilah said as she pulled the blanket tighter around her shoulders.

"Really? How so?" Susan asked.

"Well, it's just that one time he told me something like that. That certain people come into our lives and save us."

"In what way?"

"Well, he meant in a physical way."

"How so?"

"He gave me an example about someone, a stranger, stopping you on the street one day to ask for the time."

"And what? Why are they asking for the time?" Susan asked, sounding intrigued.

"To save your life, of course."

"That's an interesting idea, but can you explain to me how asking someone for the time can save that person's life?"

"Good question," Delilah said, leaning closer to her mother. "Well, the way River explained it was that in those few seconds it takes for you to give the stranger the time, it may stop you from crossing the street at the exact moment a drunk driver is zooming through a red light." Delilah looked at her mother pensively for a moment. "If that stranger didn't stop you, you would have continued on your merry way and been smashed by that car."

"I see," Susan said, looking down at her hands, seemingly in deep in thought. Delilah thought she knew what her mother was thinking.

"Mom, not everyone can be saved. I'm sure that there was a reason that Darcy wasn't saved."

"I know. I'm sure there was a reason she was taken from us so early, and I pray to God that I have that answer someday. I understand what you're saying about people being physically saved, but I also believe that there are people out there who can also save us emotionally. You know, like guardian angels."

"Who said anything about angels?" Delilah asked.

"You did. All this talk about people watching over us and protecting us somehow—D, I know that you believe in spiritual things, too, even though you sometimes pretend that you don't. I think you are more like me than you want to admit."

"Maybe, but I don't think I'm ready to delve deeper into the whole supernatural world." Delilah looked at her mother; she looked sad.

"I'm sorry if I can't be more like you, Mom, and I'm sorry I wasn't there with you the night of the séance."

"You were there with me, D. You are always here with me."

"What happened that night anyway? You didn't really say much about it other than you had some sort of epiphany that made you want to tell me about the day Darcy died."

"D, to be honest, I'm a coward. I never wanted to tell you what happened that day. I never even thought you knew about it. I would have gone on forever with that lie."

Delilah thought maybe she should be mad at her mother for telling her this, but in some ways she appreciated her honesty. "So, what? What was it that made you decide to come clean with me?"

"I don't know. I can't explain it—something just happened."

"You expect me to believe that? Who came to you? Was it Darcy?"

"No, D. Darcy didn't come to me during the séance."

"Was it Grandma?" Delilah held her breath, waiting for the answer.

"No, your grandmother didn't come through either. But it was someone's grandmother, strangely enough."

"Whose?"

"Your old pal, Rachael Nappi."

"What?" Delilah said in complete disbelief. "Are you messing with me?"

"No, it seemed very real. Her name came through to us."

"You mean to tell me that Rachael's grandmother came through to you at the séance?"

"Well, not to me exactly; she came through to Nora. Apparently she had a message for Rachael."

"Nora? Why would she say it to Nora, of all people? I mean, they're not even friends. What was the message?" *What could Rachael Nappi's grandmother want with Nora?* Rachael loved her grandmother. The only times she seemed somewhat normal were when she would talk about her grandmother. Rachael was truly devastated when she died. It was the one and only time Delilah saw her cry. *This is all too weird.*

"Honestly, D, I don't know what she wanted. Nora claimed to have gotten the message telepathically somehow. She heard a voice telling her what she had to do."

"Now I understand. Nora is probably trying to use this as a way to get in with Rachael. Wow, that's really pathetic. She's probably making the whole thing up."

"No, D, I believe her. It was a fascinating night. It would have been nice if you could have been there."

"I'm sorry, Mom, but you know how I feel about Darcy. It just scares me. And Nora and I aren't really on the best of terms."

"What happened with you and Nora? D, I just wish you would give her a chance. She really is a nice girl."

"A nice girl!" Delilah scoffed. All she can think of was how Nora cornered her in the girls' bathroom the other day and started freaking out about her relationship with the Imitators. "Mom, I'm only going to say this one more time—she's not as nice as you think. The girl definitely has some issues."

"Whatever, D. I'm just telling you what happened."

"Actually, Mom, you're not telling me what happened. I want to know who came through to you! Who made you decide to be honest with me and tell me about what really happened the morning Darcy died?"

"D, did I ever tell you about the other times your sister came through to me?"

"So it was her—Darcy, I mean. She's the one who came through to you and told you to tell the truth."

"She's come through to me before. Usually I can hear her voice. I remember the very first time it happened. It was only two days after she died and I was lying on her bed holding her pillow. I had my nose to it and I could still smell the strawberry shampoo that I had washed her hair with only a few days before. I just lay there talking to her, telling her how sorry I was about what happened."

"Did she know that you told Daddy that I was the one who didn't latch the door?"

"Yes, she knows. She knows everything. She seems so much more lucid now."

"You mean when she … speaks to you … she isn't like she was?" Delilah asked hesitantly. This is the first time Delilah talked about this with her mother, and it felt strange.

"Oh, Delilah, she's so beautiful and happy, and she's well. She smiles and speaks to me. That's actually all we used to do—speak. Until one day … one day, I got to see her."

"You saw her? When? How?" Delilah asked, feeling full of mixed emotions.

"About a year ago. I don't get to see her a lot. Usually I can just hear her voice."

"Why do you think she lets you see her?" Delilah asked, thinking of the image she saw in her mirror.

"I think it's because she knew that I really needed her. It was on a night when your dad and I had a really bad argument—one of our many bad arguments, I should say. But on this particular night

I had to fight harder than usual to quell the urge to drink. I was an emotional wreck. I physically felt like I couldn't go on without a drink. I remember walking over to my closet where I had a bottle of vodka stowed behind some old shoeboxes." As Delilah listened to her mother speak, she felt an overwhelming pang of guilt. She realized that she has been so consumed with everything going on at school that she never saw how hard this has been on her mother.

"So, what happened?" Delilah asked gently.

"What happened was she was there for me, and D, she looked so beautiful. At first I thought I was hallucinating."

"How did she look?" Delilah asked.

"She looked the same. The only difference was her eyes."

"What about her eyes?"

"Her eyes were lighter. It was almost as if I could stare right through them. She was such a sight. I didn't want her to go, but right after she left, I flushed all that vodka down the toilet. And I never looked back."

"So she was able to help you?"

"Yes, she was. Sometimes help comes from people that we least expect. In my case my help came from Darcy. She's my angel. But I'm sure there are plenty of people who have angels in their lives helping them in other ways, even if they don't know it."

"What are you trying to say, Mom?"

"I'm not trying to say anything … but it wasn't Darcy who told me to tell you the truth about the day your sister died, and I have a feeling that it wasn't really Rachael Nappi's grandmother who came through to Nora."

"What are you saying, Mom? You think the person who came through to you is the same person who came through to Nora?"

"Yes, I do, and I think it's for the same reason — to help you. D, I believe that you have your own guardian angel. Someone who cares about you a great deal. Someone who is trying to help you get your life together."

"You think you know who it is, don't you?"

"Yes, I do. I knew from the moment I met him."

"Met who? Mom, what are you talking about?"

"I'm talking about … River."

"What about River?"

"The first time I met him, I knew … I felt it."

"What are you talking about? What did you feel?"

"When I shook his hand I just knew, and then I saw it in his eyes. The same look that your sister had when she came to me."

"I can't sit here and listen to this," Delilah said as she jumped up from the couch to get away from Susan.

"He was talking to her, you know."

Delilah stopped and turned to face her mother.

"When we heard voices in the hall, he wasn't on his phone. He was talking to *her*."

"Talking to whom?" Delilah asked.

"Your sister!"

"Mom, you're scaring me. River is alive. Darcy is dead. The world can see River. *I* can see River. He doesn't evaporate into thin air when he finishes talking to me."

"Maybe it's like you said, some people can see their guardian angels. Have you ever been around him with other people from his family?"

"What? No, but what does that mean? Other people who are not his family see him."

"Yes, but what are they seeing? Maybe you see River as he was when he was alive, but what is everyone else seeing?"

"I'm not going to listen to this. You're completely out of your mind — "

"I've read about things like this before. Please just think about it. Have you ever been around someone who knew him? I don't mean strangers. I mean people in his family, friends that he's had for a while."

"I don't know, Mom."

"Well, think about it."

"Well, I guess I never have been around his family while he was there. We went to his uncle's apartment once, but no one was home. In fact, we did see the doorman at his uncle's building."

"Are you sure the doorman knew who he was? What did he say?"

"Well ..."

"What? What is it?" Her mother asked, nervously.

"It's just that he called River by his uncle's last name, Mr. Carter. River said it was because the doorman just assumed that because he was Mr. Carter's nephew they would have the same name."

"It's just like what I read. The spirits can conjure themselves up to look like other people. River could be standing in front of both you and the doorman, and to you he looks like the River you know, while to the doorman he looks like his uncle."

"Jesus, Mom. It's not like I don't have enough going on in my life right now. Do you really have to start messing with my mind? What's wrong with you?"

"There's nothing wrong with me. In fact, for the very first time in my life, I'm starting to see everything really clearly. There really is a whole other world out there beyond the life we know, and

I'm so grateful that someone came to save you, Delilah. Someone came to save my other baby."

"Really, Mom? Are you actually going to make this about you?"

"No, but I think that you really needed someone, someone to come into your life and help you. I'm sorry if I couldn't be the one to be there for you, but I'm so grateful that there was someone there for you—an angel!"

"An angel?"

"Yes, D, there is a reason you are here, and a reason you are supposed to stay here. I believe that River was sent to help you. I'm sure it was him at the séance. He's the one who told me to tell you the truth, and I think he has something planned for Rachael. He told Nora to go to school and tell Rachael what happened."

"What? Mom this is crazy. I want to believe that you've stopped drinking, but when you act like this—"

"Don't do that! Please don't talk to me like I'm crazy. I think I have more sense than most people. God, D, look at the world we live in. Don't you think there's more to it than just this? I sure as hell hope so."

"I hope so too, Mom. Really, I do. And I know how much it means to you to believe that there really is life after death, but acting like this—it just scares me. Please, just stop it," Delilah said as she reached out and held her mother's hands. "I love you, but I have to go now. I'm going to take your car." Susan put her head in her hands and then quickly looked up as if she just remembered something.

"D, you know that you're not supposed to be driving without a licensed driver."

"Mom, I'll be fine. I'll see you later."

"Oh, and D, I invited your dad for dinner this weekend. We can have that talk with him then."

"Okay," Delilah said as she grabbed her mother's car keys from the table and headed out the door. She started to call River as she walked to the car, but before she finished dialing, her phone started to ring.

"Hi."

"I need to see you right away," River said. His voice sounded urgent.

"Is everything okay?" Delilah asked, a bit nervous.

"Listen, where are you now?" River asked frantically.

"I'm in front of my house. I was just about to come and meet you."

"Stay where you are. I'm coming over now."

"River?" she said, but he had already hung up.

Delilah walked back into the house and found her mother sitting at the dining room table drinking a bottle of water.

"What are you doing back?" Susan asked, looking surprised to see her.

"I just spoke to River and he's on his way over to see me."

"Oh, then I will leave you two alone," she said. Delilah realized that her mother must really believe that River was an angel. Otherwise she would never offer to leave them alone.

"Where will you go?"

"I was thinking of going over to see your father," she said nervously, sounding like a woman about to go on a first date.

"You're not going to say anything about Darcy, are you?"

"No, I promised you that I wouldn't say anything about that until we are all together."

"Thank you. Well, I'm going to freshen up before River gets here." Delilah headed toward her room, then stopped and turned to face her mother. "Mom, I love you."

Susan smiled. "I love you, too, sweetheart." As Delilah left the room, Susan whispered to herself, "You'll never know how much."

Delilah quickly brushed her teeth and swished some mouthwash. She brushed her hair, applied a few coats of mascara, and put on some lip gloss. She ran to unlock the front door, and sat on the couch with a magazine, trying to make herself look as calm as possible, even though she was a pile of nerves on the inside.

River knocked gently on the door.

"Come in. The door is open."

"You know it's not safe to leave your front door unlocked," River said with a smile, closing and locking the door behind him.

"I knew you were coming over. I figured I would just take my chances," she said as she gets up from the sofa and throws her arms around him. He squeezed her back. It felt so good to be in his arms. She started to cry.

"What's the matter?" he asked softly.

"I think you already know," Delilah said as she stepped away from him and started pacing the floor.

"Talk to me," River whispered.

"I'm sorry. I'm so sorry. I went to see your father today."

"I imagine that you must have some questions for me then," River said calmly.

"Yes, I guess you can say that."

"It must have been pretty strange for you, meeting my father."

"It was. I hope you know that I didn't go there with the intention of hurting you. I just thought that maybe I could bring the two of you together. I have to be honest with you, River, from the things you told me about your mother, I couldn't help but think that she may have purposely created the distance between you and your father."

"And you thought that if you went there today that you might be able to patch things up?"

"Yes, I'm sorry. Things didn't go at all according to my plan."

"Things haven't exactly gone according to my plan either," River mumbled under his breath. "So what did my father tell you about me?" he asked Delilah.

"Well, um ... he really didn't say much," Delilah lied. She didn't want to risk hurting him by telling him that his father thinks he's dead.

"Please, tell me what he said to you."

"He said that you ... well, that you ... died. I mean, at first I just assumed that it was a lie your mother told him, but now I know it's something he's just pretending to believe. I'm not sure why he's doing it, but River, I'm really sorry. You don't need those people. It's obvious they aren't any good."

"Please don't say that! I should have known that you were too smart and too caring to just let something like this go. I know that you went down there today because you care about me."

"River, I love you. I'm sorry that I haven't told you sooner. You've helped me to realize that life can be good again and that I have self-worth. I can't tell you what having you in my life has meant to me."

"Delilah, I want to do more for you if you'll let me. You need to know that there's a reason you're here, and you should never, ever question your self-worth again. Your life is so precious. It just hurts me to think that you would ever try to—"

"Try to what?" She could hardly get the words out.

"You know what you tried to do to yourself."

"I *never* told you about that. What is this about, River? Have you been speaking to my mother?"

"You know, despite everything, your mother loves you so much."

"Despite what?" Delilah asked. River looked at her intently. She stared into his eyes and she could see right through them. They were transparent, just like her mother described Darcy's eyes. For the first time, Delilah could see his eyes as they really were. "You! It was you who told my mother to come clean about Darcy's accident. So it's true? What are you?"

"I'm your friend … a Divine One," he said with a beautiful smile.

"That's it? That's all you have to say? And all this time, you're the real imitator. Impersonating a real person–a person who can eat, bleed, and more importantly, impersonating a person who cares about me."

"Cares about you? Delilah, I love you. You see, Delilah, I picked you."

"Picked me? For what?"

"For my assignment. I must admit there were a lot of reasons why I picked you. For one, you are so beautiful, and I could feel all the pain you were feeling. I knew a lot of it had to do with your sister—your Darcy. Once I learned your sister had the same name as mine, I knew that it was fate and that you were the one I had to help."

"Help me? Is this help? I feel like I'm losing my mind."

"No, you're not. You're fine. You're probably one of the most lucid people I've ever known."

"So my sister, Darcy—you can speak with her?" Delilah asked without hesitation.

"Yes, I can. I spoke with her the very first time I was at your house. She's a very sweet girl, and she loves you very much." Delilah looked into River's eyes and tried to speak, but she couldn't. She began to feel lightheaded and unsteady and she started to stumble backward.

River grabbed her and helped her onto the couch. He sat down next to her and held her hand. "I wanted to be completely honest with you right from the beginning."

"So everything you've told me has been a lie? You were never raised in Florida by a drug addict and you don't have a brother and a couple of nephews?"

"What I told you about my mother is true, and I do have a half-brother named Josh, but no, I wasn't raised by him. He went to live with his grandparents when he was very young."

"So if you weren't living with your brother Josh and his family — which, by the way, I kind of figured out wasn't the complete truth when I saw the same names of your nephews and sister-in-law in the aquarium brochure — who were you living with?"

"I'm sorry about that. I did have to make up some things on the fly and I hated to lie to you. It's just what I had to do to protect you. I wasn't living with my brother. I was living with my father. We just thought it would be better if you thought I was from out of town and I was just here visiting family."

"You mean you were raised by Robert Spencer?"

"Yes, I was."

"And what happened to your mother, the one you told me all those terrible stories about? Whatever happened to her? And what did you mean when you said, 'we thought it would be better'? Who do you mean by 'we'?"

"Delilah, there is so much more I want to tell you. So much more I wish that I could tell you. The 'we' is my counselor and I. That's what we call them. They're kind of like our mentors. The people who help us to make our transition after we cross over."

"Cross over?"

"Yes, D—and in answer to your question about my mother, she's dead. She's buried at the Furlong Cemetery in Florida."

"What happened to her?"

"I shot her after she murdered me."

Chapter 11

"I'm so sorry to lay all of this on you. I had no intention of it being this way, but I didn't know that you were going to go down and see my father. I also didn't realize that your mom had the gift."

"You mean the gift to speak to the dead? You know, most girls hope that their mothers can hit it off with their boyfriends, so I guess I'm actually lucky that my boyfriend happens to be a ghost and my mother's a medium!" she said sarcastically.

"Delilah, do you remember when I told you about guardian angels coming into our lives when we least expect it?"

"So you're my guardian angel?"

"Yes."

"What happened to you? How did you get like this?"

"I tried to be as honest as possible with you, Delilah, and what I told you about my mother was true. Even the part about how my parents met and how my mother resented my father. She was very jealous of the relationship I had with him. One day, he was supposed to pick me up and take me to a baseball game—and he did. He picked me up and never brought me back. He took me to live with him and his wife and their baby daughter, Darcy, in Westchester, New York. It was the best thing that could have happened to me."

"His wife didn't mind that you came to live with them?"

"She's really a wonderful person. She understood that my father made a mistake, and she was willing to raise me as her own. My dad swore that he would spend the rest of his life making things right between the two of them." Delilah thought back to being in Robert's office that morning and remembered how kindly he had spoken to his wife. She guessed he was keeping his promise.

"So what happened with your mother?"

"She was crazy. She couldn't stand the fact that my father took me away from her. She tried to get custody of me, but my dad is a great lawyer with a lot of connections, so her efforts were useless. Even with her brother helping her—and Daniel Carter is another great attorney—they didn't stand a chance. To be honest, I think my uncle put on a good act for my mother, but he knew that I really belonged with my father. He just went through the legal motions to appease my mother."

"So what happened?"

"My father wasn't a cruel man. He would still take me to Florida to visit her and he always told her that if she would clean up her act he would consider joint custody, but she never did. I never completely cut her out of my life; I just wanted her to get help with her addiction." River stopped for a moment and looked at Delilah. "That's something else we have in common," he said softly. "But you're lucky your mother is beating her addiction. I really believe that she's going to be okay."

"I know," Delilah said, trying to sound optimistic. *It's frightening how much he knows about me.* Despite all the crazy events in the past few days, Delilah didn't think she had ever felt safer in her life. Even though being here with River felt completely surreal, and she was shocked by what she was hearing, she still felt protected somehow — just like she felt every time she was with him. Now she understood why.

"What happened, River? What happened between you and your mother?" Delilah asked, almost afraid to hear the answer.

"My father flew my mother up to New York for the weekend of my twenty-second birthday. She brought her friend, Norm, and the two of them stayed together at a hotel in the city. On the night of my birthday she insisted on having dinner with me alone. I agreed to meet with her first, but planned on going back to my father's house immediately after dinner. During dinner she started mumbling something about her friend Norm. I knew that she had been drinking so I didn't really pay much attention to what she was saying."

"What did she say?"

"She said that Norm really loved her and would do anything for her and that he was going to help her to make things right. I just never put the pieces together."

"How could you? She was so vague."

"After dinner was over, I went back to my father's house. When I got there the house was engulfed in flames. My father and stepmother were outside on the lawn, screaming that Darcy was still inside. My father and I ran back into the house, but the smoke was just too much for him. I ran upstairs and found my sister unconscious on her bedroom floor. I picked her up and got out of the house."

"River, you are a hero. So you got out of the house. Everything was okay," Delilah stuttered, trying to sound hopeful.

"Everything was okay for a few seconds. As I was carrying my sister over to my father, I saw a man with a gun; he was aiming it at Darcy. I quickly handed Darcy to my father and then I heard a gunshot. At that moment, I didn't know if anyone had been shot. I just ran toward the gunman and tried to wrestle the gun away. As we fought the gun went off again, multiple times. I felt a tremendous force hit me in the stomach. I tried to ignore the unrelenting pain that I was feeling and continued to try to tackle him to the ground. By the time I was able to wrestle the gun away, the police and firemen had arrived.

"As I lay there on the ground, dying, I could hear the police officers talking on their radios. They were saying that they had two gunshot victims. I remember one of my last thoughts being 'Please don't let it be my sister.' As they were taking me away on a stretcher, I looked over and saw my mother lying on the ground. She was also covered in blood. Apparently she followed me in a cab back to my father's house. She had planned on watching the whole thing. My mother wanted her friend Norm to kill my father's family by setting the house on fire, and if that didn't work, she wanted him to shoot and kill Darcy. I guess in her sick state of mind she was able to justify her actions—they took her child away, so she was going to take theirs."

"So you saved Darcy—twice—and ended up accidentally killing your own mother," Delilah said hysterically. Delilah gingerly lifted River's shirt. His skin was so pale, paler than she ever realized. She ran her hand up the front and sides of his chest. He had such a beautiful body; it feels so hard and cold. She gently ran her fingertips along the front of his stomach and felt it, the gunshot wound. She bent down and put her lips to his wound and kissed him softly. She began to sob. "You must have gone straight to heaven," she said.

"Well, you make a few stops along the way," he said, pulling her in and hugging her.

"So this whole time, from the moment we met at the coffee shop, you knew all about me?"

"Yes, and there are so many others like me. People who left this earth too early and now have jobs helping others who are needed here for a purpose. When I read your file, there were so many things about you —"

"Wait a minute. You read a file on me? There are *files* on people in the afterlife?"

"Yes. Well, kind of. That's the best way I can think to explain it so that you'll understand. And please don't call it the afterlife, because it's not. My life isn't over; it's just a different kind of life. Delilah, there really is so much that I want to tell you, but I just can't right now. I've probably told you too much already."

"Like all that stuff you told me the other day about someone stopping and asking for the time, how it could be your guardian angel protecting you from getting hit by a car? All of those things you said were true? And you're not just some guy with an abstract interest in philosophy—you really know what you're talking about. Now that I think about it, there were a lot of little clues. I feel like such an idiot."

"What other clues?" River asked.

"Like how anytime a dog crossed your path it would bark and go nuts. That was funny," Delilah said, smiling. "There is also the fact that anytime you touched me, I got shivers up and down my spine."

"Really?" River said bashfully. "Maybe that was just my charm?"

"I'm serious," Delilah said with a smile. "I just knew there was something. I just never thought anything of it, but now it makes sense. I remember my mother telling me that the room gets colder when there's a spiritual presence."

"Your mother knew about me from the first moment she met me."

"You knew that?" Delilah asked, sounding surprised.

"Yes. I also knew that she knew it was me the night of the séance, but she never faltered. She listened to what I had to say and she complied."

"That's right. The night of the séance you were here. God, I feel like such a fool. I believed that I had a boyfriend who was at some corporate event, meanwhile …"

"Please, Delilah. There is no reason for you to feel like that. How could you have known? Believe me, everything will make more sense to you when it's your time, but your time isn't now. There are things you have to do here first. Things your children have to do."

"Children? Who said anything about children?"

"Well, one day when you get married and start a family, you're going to have children. Very special children."

"Wait a minute! Get married? How can you talk to me like this? River, I love you! Don't you realize that you're breaking my heart? I mean, what did you think was going to happen? You would just come into my life and make everything all better, and I wouldn't feel anything for you?"

"I'm sorry. I can't help what I feel for you, too, Delilah. I'm still a man, and I do love you—very, very much. Being here with you was the only way that I could truly help you. There was only so much that I could do without physically being with you."

"So you were there with me during some of the hard times?"

"Yes, I was."

"I knew it. On that night, the night I took that bottle of pills. All those images of my family, all those happy memories—that was you?"

"I had to stop you from doing something so foolish. You just weren't thinking clearly."

"I know. I can't explain it now, but I just felt so lost at the time. I guess you already know all there is to know about me. And all this time I thought we were really starting a relationship. I even began to confide in you, and the whole time you already knew everything—everything! My God, did you even watch me while I showered?"

"No, that would be against the rules. Although I wouldn't mind at all if that was part of the job," River said, trying to break the tension.

"This isn't a joke. Was anything real? How about when we met in the park and you were attacked?"

"I needed a way to prove to you that you were stronger than you thought so you would see that you can handle your life. You can handle this. You just needed a little reminding."

"A little reminding? My God, so everything has been fake."

"No, not everything. Delilah, I love you. I had to help you get your life back on track."

"And my mother's séance? Was that about helping me?"

"Yes. I needed to get through to your mother, and that was the best way for me to do it. I needed for her to tell you that what happened to your sister wasn't your fault."

"Do you think you made things better? My mother feels awful. She didn't even know that I overheard her and my dad talking that night."

"She was still living with a lie," River said adamantly. "It was eating away at her. I did her a favor. I know she feels better for having confessed what she did. Now the ball is in your court: you have the information and you can do what you want with it."

"What's that supposed to mean? Are you saying that I shouldn't tell my dad the truth?"

"I'm not saying anything. We all have free will; you do what you want with it."

"I will," Delilah said, trying to sound confident. "So what's next? My mother said something about Rachael's grandmother coming through in the séance. What is that all about?"

"Trust me," River said, nudging her on the shoulder.

"I do trust you, River. I think I trust you more than I've ever trusted anyone in my life." He reached out to her. She tried to fight the urge to reach out to him, but her attempt is futile. She grabbed him and held him close. He kissed her lips and she felt the usual shiver run up and down her spine, but more intensely this time. She didn't want to let go. "I love you," she said.

Chapter 12

Delilah didn't know how she managed to pull herself together to go to school the next day but, despite everything, she had faith in River and she found that he was true to his word—as soon as she got to school, she saw Nora in the hallway talking with Rachael, Emily, and the other Imitators. Delilah hid around the corner and strained her ears to listen while they spoke.

"What the hell are you talking about, you little freak?" Rachael snapped. "Are you trying to tell me that my dead grandmother spoke to you during some random séance? What are you, schizophrenic?"

"No, of course not, but … Rachael, it's true."

"Do you know that I was raised by my grandmother until I was thirteen years old?"

"No, I didn't, but—"

"Well then maybe you don't know how much she meant to me or how devastated I was when she died! I don't appreciate anyone making a mockery of her death! Do you understand me?" Rachael said venomously.

"Rachael, the last thing I want to do is mock you or your grandmother. She told me to tell you that she wants to speak with you and that she has a message for you."

"I'm supposed to believe that? God, you're so weird!" Rachael said.

"I'm telling you the truth. You have to believe me," Nora pleaded. "She wants me to organize a séance and—"

"Come on Rach, let's just go," Natalie interrupted.

"So you're telling me that my grandmother wants you to have a séance? You're such a little freak. I should beat the crap out of you right here and now."

"Come on, Rachael, just lay off her. She probably has some issues," Charlotte interjected, trying to rectify the situation.

"Charlotte, shut up. I've had it up to here,"— Rachael lifted her hand to her forehead—"with your holier-than-thou attitude. Let's just go."

As Rachael walked away, Nora yelled out to her. "Your grandmother wanted me to tell you to stop picking punk from between your toes."

"Ew!" The other girls begin to laugh.

"This is it, poor Nora is going to get punched in the face," Charlotte said in a loud whisper.

"What did you say?" Rachael said, walking back to Nora and standing nose-to-nose with her. "I asked you what you just said!"

Nora takes a step back and swallows hard. "She said that you better stop picking punk—you know, the fuzzy stuff that socks sometimes leave behind—and ..."

"I know what you mean by 'punk.' What I don't know is how you knew that. That was a joke between my grandmother and me. Tell me how you knew that!"

"I told you, Rachael, I'm not lying. She wanted me to organize a séance. She said there's more that she has to tell you."

As Delilah stood in the hall watching this spectacle, she couldn't help but feel sorry for Nora. She was just an innocent pawn in this whole thing. River really did communicate with Rachael's grandmother. Apparently, she has been so disappointed with Rachael's behavior that she was willing to do just about anything to help get her back on track, including giving River a little inside information, which he passed along to Nora as evidence that her grandmother had come through in the séance.

"Yeah, all right. Where should we do this thing?" Rachael asked Nora.

"We can have it at my house this weekend. I can make popcorn and order a pizza," Nora said, trying to take advantage of the situation.

"Um, you can forget about the pizza. We are not hanging out and I better not find out that you are using this as a way to improve your social status. And I don't want to wait until this weekend — we'll do it at your house tonight!"

"Okay, but, um, there was one other thing. She wanted Delilah Simms to be there too."

"What?" Rachael snapped.

"What?" Delilah unwittingly said aloud. She quickly covered her mouth with her hands.

"I haven't discussed it with Delilah yet so I don't know what she's going to say, but your grandmother made it very clear to me that she wanted Delilah to be present at the séance."

"This whole thing is getting weirder and weirder! But I have to admit you piqued my interest. I'm not going to take any chances just in case there is some truth to this, but I'm telling you right now — there better be no funny business, and I won't be coming alone. I'll have a few of the girls there with me."

"What about Delilah?" Nora asked, sounding terrified.

"Well, if my dearly departed grandmother wants her there, then you better figure out a way to get her there!" Rachael said snidely as she turned and walked away.

After Rachael left, Delilah walked over to Nora, who was still standing in the same spot.

"Oh Delilah, I have to talk to you and you're not going to believe it but—"

"I heard," Delilah interrupted. "I heard the whole thing. You need me at your house tonight to take part in a séance for Rachael's grandmother." As Delilah said the words, she still couldn't believe it.

"That's right," Nora said timidly. "So will you do it?"

As much as Delilah wanted to say no, she knew this was what River wanted and she didn't have much of a choice. "Yes, fine, I will be there."

"Thank you, Delilah," Nora said sincerely. "To be honest, if I were you I don't know if I would go, especially since it's for Rachael Nappi."

"Nora, I've been doing a lot of things lately that I didn't think I would ever do." Delilah thought about her conversation with River's father. "Listen, I have to get to class before I'm really late. Just call me with the details."

As soon as Delilah got home from school, she called River. She wanted to know what he was up to and why he told Nora that she had to attend the séance—but he didn't answer his phone. Delilah began to have second thoughts and questioned whether she should go at all. As she sat in her room and thought about what she should do, the phone rang; it was Nora. She told Delilah that everyone would be meeting at her house at eight o'clock that night. When Delilah hung up the phone, she was surprised that she didn't have her usual nervous feeling. Instead, she felt empowered somehow. For the first time, she didn't have any doubt. She knew that this was something that had to be done. She had to be there.

Delilah knocked on Nora's door at eight o'clock sharp; Nora's mother, Claire, greeted her.

"Hello, Delilah, dear, I'm so glad you could make it," Claire said excitedly. She had always wanted her daughter to be popular, so all the Imitators meeting at their house was really thrilling for her. The fact that there was a séance must have really sweetened the pot.

"Hello, Mrs. Peterson," Delilah said with a grin.

"All the girls are already here. They are downstairs in the basement. Nora and I set everything up earlier—the card table, Ouija Board, candles. There's even a stocked fridge down there."

"Thanks, Mrs. Peterson. That was really nice of you," Delilah said as she hung her coat on the oversized coat rack standing in the corner of the entranceway.

"Delilah, are you all right? I mean, I know that you have been having a hard time with the girls who are here tonight."

"Yes, you could definitely say that," Delilah said.

"Well, maybe this is your chance to make everything better, and you girls can stop all this nonsense and be friends again," she said optimistically.

"I'm not the one who needs to make things better," Delilah said sternly. "They are the ones who did something wrong. And as far as being friends with them, there is only one girl down there that I would ever talk to again, and right now she doesn't want anything to do with me."

"Well then … ahem," Claire cleared her throat. "Don't forget to help yourself to whatever is in the fridge," she said, looking frazzled.

"Will do," Delilah said, waving her hand back at Claire as she headed down the basement stairs. As Delilah came down the stairs she couldn't believe her eyes. The basement looked like a gypsy lived there. The windows were covered with long beads, there were candles everywhere, and in the center of the room there was a large round table covered with a black tablecloth. In the middle of the table there was an array of paraphernalia. From where she was standing, Delilah only recognized the Ouija board and a deck of tarot cards. There were also what seemed to be colorful stones or gems spread out on the table. *River must be getting a kick out of this.* Sitting around the table were Rachael, Charlotte, Emily, Natalie, and Nora. She was wearing a red afghan around her shoulders. Delilah couldn't believe how much she was immersing herself in the role.

"Look who decided to grace us with her presence," Rachael snapped when she saw Delilah approaching the table.

"Just leave it alone Rachael," Charlotte said timidly.

"And lucky for you I decided to grace you with my presence," Delilah said.

"What's that supposed to mean?" Rachael shrieked.

"It means that spending my evening with you isn't my idea of a fun-filled night. I'm only doing this because I'm curious," Delilah said, trying to sound convincing.

"Well would you mind turning around and looking at the wall? I really don't like the idea of having to stare at a back-stabbing bitch!"

"What did you call me?" Delilah yelled. *Think of how you smashed that guy in the face with the brick and how you were able to confront River's father. You can do this!* "You are the back-stabbing bitch! You are nothing but a troublemaker and a liar, and if you just give me the chance, I would love to —"

"Oh, please! Delilah, I love this newfound confidence of yours," Rachael said mockingly. "But it's not going to do you any good. Are you forgetting you have a horrible reputation with the entire senior class? What are you going to do, confront everyone?"

"No! You are!" a strange voice said, and everyone jumped. The candles began to flicker on and off.

"Who … who said that?" Rachael stuttered.

"I did!" The words were coming out of Nora's mouth, but it wasn't Nora's voice. Nora's eyes rolled into the back of her head. Charlotte, Emily, and Natalie looked like they were about to pass out.

"Nora, if you are faking this whole thing, I swear I'll get even with you," Natalie said.

"Tonight isn't about getting even. It's about setting the record straight. And that's where you come in, my dear granddaughter Rachael!"

"My God, Grandma it … it sounds just like you, but how do I know this isn't a trick?"

"Rachael, my little *babushka*. Remember I used to call you that?"

"Yes, I do." Rachael's eyes began to tear.

"Now, did you ever tell any of these girls that I called you that? Or that I used to tease you about picking the punk from between your toes?" Nora continued to speak in the voice that only Rachael seemed to recognize.

"No, I don't think I ever said anything about any of it," Rachael cried.

"Well, there's something else I know you never told them — something only you and I know about. Do you remember what I told you right before I died — you know, about living by the Golden Rule?"

"Yes, you told me to treat others the way that I would want to be treated."

"And …"

"You also told me to have respect for myself," Rachael said, her voice quivering.

"And …"

"You said that no guy would buy the cow if you gave the milk out for free."

"Well, then, that wasn't so hard. I'm glad you were paying attention. Now, I don't have much time. You need to set things right with these girls. You need to tell the truth. It will be hard for you at first, but you are my brave *babushka*, and I know that you will do the right thing and make me proud of you once again. Please, Rachael, make this right! Remember, I love you always."

For a moment there was silence.

"So, when we start the séance, I will ask a question and then we will go around and — what? What's wrong with everyone?" Nora asked, looking completely baffled.

"Nora, don't you know what just happened?" Delilah asked.

"What? What just happened?" Nora asked, looking as clueless as ever.

"It was my grandmother! She … she came through. I never thought I would believe it, but the things that she knew, the voice — it was her!"

"Are you trying to tell me that your grandmother possessed my body? That is so … so … amazingly cool!"

"Give it a rest, Nora," Emily said.

"Rachael, are you all right?" Charlotte asked, sounding concerned.

"Yes, I'm all right," Rachael said through tears. "But I have something that I want to say to you Charlotte." Rachael's voice didn't even sound like her own. Instead of her usual confident, cocky voice, she sounded meek and insecure. "I'll make it short and sweet. Delilah never slept with Steve —

she never even kissed him. I just tried to make it look like she did so the two of you would stop talking. I actually did a lot of things that I shouldn't have, just to cause problems between you two. I guess I let the whole thing get out of control and I'm sorry. Delilah, I'm sorry to you, too. I guess I was pretty shitty to you. Charlotte, I just want to say—" Rachael was interrupted by Charlotte's hand slapping her in the face. Charlotte didn't even face Delilah. She just got up and ran up the stairs. Emily, Natalie, and Nora sat there with their mouths open.

"So, what are you going to do now?" Emily asked Rachael.

"I think you better tell a lot of other people this same confession," Natalie said.

"Don't worry—I can let my friends know," Nora chimed in.

"Well, that takes care of two people, now how are you going to spread the word to everyone else?" Emily said to Rachael. Natalie looked at Emily and gave a disapproving glance.

"You just better make this right, Rachael," Delilah said irately.

"I will, Delilah. I promise I will," Rachael said, sounding desperate.

Delilah sat there for a moment looking at Rachael, stone-faced. Then she stood up and walked toward the stairs.

The next day at school quite a few people came up to Delilah to apologize for having thought such bad things about her. Delilah was gracious and told them that it was okay. She knew from that moment on that the rest of her senior year wouldn't be so bad. There was still one thing that was missing, though — her friend Charlotte. Charlotte was absent from school, so Delilah didn't have an opportunity to speak with her. She didn't know how Charlotte was going to handle the whole situation. She guessed that Charlotte just needed some time to digest everything, but Delilah didn't know how much time she was willing to give her. Now that Charlotte knew the truth, the ball was in her court.

Delilah's doorbell rang at nine o'clock that evening. She hoped that it was River. She hadn't spoken to him since he told her he was preparing for the séance with Rachael. When she opened the door, she saw Charlotte standing there. She was wearing an old T-shirt and a pair of flannel pajama bottoms. Her hair was in a tight ponytail and her eyes were completely swollen and puffy; it looked as if she had been crying all day. Delilah saw a cab parked behind her in the driveway.

"You called a cab?" Delilah said.

"Well did you expect me to run over to apologize?" she said, trying to be flippant. If anyone ever heard a conversation between Charlotte and Delilah when they were best friends, they would probably have thought that they hated each other. Charlotte and Delilah liked to banter back and forth, in a loving way.

"Of course not—you were never athletic," Delilah said.

"Look who's talking."

"Are you forgetting I won the blue ribbon in sixth grade for jumping hurdles?" Delilah asked with a smirk.

"Are you still talking about that blue ribbon? I can see I haven't missed much." They both started to laugh, and just like that, they were friends again.

"Are you going to let me inside so you can tell me what's new with you?"

"Isn't your meter running?" Delilah asked.

"No, I paid him. I just asked him to wait two minutes. I wasn't sure if you would slam the door in my face or not, so I needed a back-up plan. He'll drive off in a second," Charlotte said with a laugh.

Charlotte and Delilah talked a lot that night, but Delilah never mentioned River. She figured that she would just wait for Charlotte to meet him herself. Thinking about it later, Delilah realized that was probably a bit naïve.

At around twelve thirty AM, Delilah heard a knock on her front door. She jumped up and ran to answer it, trying not to wake her mother. She looked through the peephole. River was standing on the other side.

"Can't you just walk through doors?" Delilah asked while pressing her lips to the door.

"Actually, I can, but I thought that would be rude," River said with a nervous laugh. "Now open the door." Delilah could tell from his voice that something was wrong. She quickly opened the door.

"What's the matter with you?" she asked anxiously.

"Nothing. I just came to see how you're feeling. I couldn't stop thinking about you all night. I'm so happy that you and Charlotte were able to patch things up tonight."

"How did you know?" Delilah asked skeptically. "I was going to wait until morning to tell you all about it, but I forgot that you have your ways of already knowing," she said with a grin. "It's weird though, you know with Charlotte and me, even after all we've been through, it still feels like nothing has changed."

"That's good, Delilah, really. I'm happy for you. Have you decided what you're going to do about your father yet? Are you going to tell him the truth about your mom?"

"You seem to know me better than I know myself. What do you think?"

"I think that you're going to have to make that decision for yourself when you have the opportunity." Delilah could tell River already knew what she was going to do.

"Listen, Delilah, we don't have a lot of time. I just wanted to tell you —"

"What do you mean we don't have a lot of time? You should have more time than anyone I know."

"Delilah, you're a smart girl. What do you think? We can just keep going on like this? You do realize that to the rest of the world I'm dead, right? I have to change my appearance in front of anyone who knew me before."

"I know, but ..."

"And did you really think we could go on like that?"

"What are you saying, River? You're scaring me."

"What I'm saying is that I have to go. I should have left already. I am literally on borrowed time."

"Borrowed time? What do you mean?"

"I actually borrowed time from one of the other …," he hesitated for a moment, "well, Divine Ones, that's what they call us. They are sort of like my co-workers, you might say. We are each given a certain amount of time to try and do our job, and I've done my job, D. You're doing great. I should have left yesterday, but I just couldn't bring myself to get to this point."

"What point?" Her voice was uneven.

"The point where I have to say good-bye to you."

"What? Why?"

"I just explained to you why."

"I know. I know everything you're saying makes sense, but a part of me thought that being with you meant never having to say good-bye. I mean, the scariest part of loving someone so much is the risk of losing them, but you already died, so I just thought that …"

"That what? You would have me around forever?"

"I guess. I know it sounds stupid, but I just thought you would always be in my life."

"Did you expect that we would get married someday, too?"

"I don't know. Now you're making fun of me. I'm sorry if I'm naïve — this is just all new to me."

"You mean the being in love with a ghost thing, right?"

"Yes, and this isn't funny!"

"I'm sorry. I'm just trying to lighten the mood. The last thing I would ever want to do is make fun of you. I love you, Delilah."

"I love you, too. I can't … I just can't say good-bye to you. How can I say good-bye to someone who has saved my life in so many ways?" She could feel herself approaching hysteria.

"I was just doing what I had to do."

"Don't do that. Please don't make me feel like just one of your assignments."

"You know that's not the case. That was never the case with you. I always knew that you were special, and I knew this was going to happen. Delilah, from the first moment I met you I felt this connection between us."

"River, I—oh my God, what's happening?" As Delilah spoke to River she could see him starting to fade right in front of her eyes.

"Delilah, I told you that I was on borrowed time. That's the way it works. I need you to know that I love you, and you were never just an assignment. You are so special. I don't want you to ever forget that."

"River, please!" she screamed. "I want to be with you."

"No! Your place is here. You have too many important things that you have to do. I know you don't believe it now, but you will fall in love again, and you will be very, very, happy."

"But I want you to be happy, too," she said, sobbing. At that moment she knew just how much River meant to her. She didn't even care if she had him, just as long as she knew that he was happy.

"Delilah, I am happy. I am so happy. I get to watch over all the people I love most in the world and protect them. When the time is right, I'll see all my loved ones again."

"What about me?" she asked desperately.

"Yes, we'll see each other again." He was little more than a shadow now.

"Will it be the same? Will we be the same?"

"Yes, I will still be in love with you. Nothing will have changed for me. Nothing ever will." It was the last thing he said before he disappeared from her life.

Chapter 13

After a full month of crying herself to sleep, Delilah finally began to realize that she would never see or hear from River again, at least not in this lifetime. She had no way to contact him. She had even gone to his uncle's law firm, the law firm where he never actually worked. She didn't know what to expect. She just hoped that maybe she would see him again, if only for a second. His phone was dead. She couldn't even listen to his voicemail. It was as if he just fell off the earth—and in a way, he did.

Delilah's mother was very comforting; she helped her to work through the pain. Delilah knew that her mother had been feeling better ever since her father moved back in. Delilah was glad to have him living with them again.

Delilah and her mother never did tell him the truth about Darcy's accident. Her mother kept her end of the bargain and invited him over for dinner, but when Delilah had the opportunity to say what really happened, she just couldn't do it. She realized that no good would come out of telling him the truth. Her mother was right. Her father loved her unconditionally, and he believed that it was an accident. If she were to tell him about her mother, he would blame the alcohol, and he would never forgive her. That guilt could easily drive Susan to drink again. Delilah knew that she couldn't let that happen. Her parents seemed happy again, and that made her happy. They even talked about planning a second honeymoon to Hawaii.

For some reason, ever since River left, Susan was no longer able to connect with Darcy in the same way. She thought it was because her soul was at peace. Susan still talked to Darcy from time to time, just in case she's still listening. Delilah liked to think that Darcy was with River. She liked to imagine the two of them helping other people.

Things were a lot better for Delilah at school. Rachael Nappi's popularity had plummeted and her whole personality seemed to have changed overnight. She had become really quiet and kept to herself more. Delilah also heard that she studied a lot and had become a much better student—her grandmother was probably happy.

Delilah knew that she would always have a place in her heart for River and that she would never forget what he did for her. She knew now that he was there with her on that desperate night she tried to take her own life, and he was there for her when she needed him again. He saved her both physically and emotionally. At times, Delilah thought about what he meant when he said that each person has a purpose here on Earth, and some need to stay here longer, while others need to leave to serve a greater purpose someplace else. Delilah guessed she would understand someday why she needed to be saved. Someday she would understand. Someday.

Epilogue

"Look at her, sitting there with her grandchildren. She seemed so happy, so content. I still love her, you know.

"I know you do. Almost sixty-five years after you saved her, and you still look at my sister like she's the same seventeen-year-old beauty she used to be—not an eighty-two-year-old woman with gray hair and wrinkles."

"She's still beautiful to me. No matter how many cases I've had after her, she was the only one I ever loved. I'm so proud of her and her family."

"I'm proud of her, too. She's been an excellent mother and grandmother."

"She had to be to raise two such exceptional daughters."

"I am very proud of my nieces. Two scientists making great strides in medicine."

"I know you must be especially proud of your niece, Ella, naming her foundation after you."

"I am so proud that she has been able to help so many children that have problems like I had."

"I wish she could see you now," River said with a smile.

"She'll see me again. And you."

"You know she asked me right before I left if things would be the same when we saw each other again. I tried to answer her without lying."

"What did you say?"

"I told her that things would be the same for me, and they will be. I didn't have the heart to tell her that things wouldn't be the same for her. I know she'll be happy to be reunited with her husband of almost fifty years, but that's not what she needed to hear at seventeen."

"My sister will still be happy to see you, and I know she'll be so grateful to you for helping her to have such a wonderful life."

CPSIA information can be obtained at www.ICGtesting.com
Printed in the USA
BVOW11s2107260814

364355BV00010B/182/P